Jacob had first s̲[...]
over a rise far do̲[...] and then as quickly
disappear. He kept walking, swinging his huge
flashlight as he went, expecting them to reappear
at any moment. Not that it mattered. The car was
heading the wrong way for him anyhow, even if by
some miracle it was someone who would consider
giving him a ride. At least it had stopped snowing.
Just then the beam of his flashlight caught a car
sitting in the darkness. There were people inside.
He hesitated a moment. What if it were a trick? For
himself he didn't mind dying. Lord knew he was
ready to go, but Arlene needed him now. He had
to get to Washington. Yet here, perhaps, was
somebody else in need. He started across the road,
heading for the driver's side of the car.

Katherine Paterson

Katherine Paterson was born in China, the daughter of missionary parents. Educated both there and in the United States, she is the author of a number of books for young adults, including THE GREAT GILLY HOPKINS and BRIDGE TO TERA-BITHIA. She lives in Barre, Vermont with her husband and four children.

STAR OF NIGHT

Stories for Christmas

Katherine Paterson

HODDER AND STOUGHTON
LONDON SYDNEY AUCKLAND TORONTO

Copyright © 1979 by Katherine
Paterson

First published in the USA as
Angels and Other Strangers

This edition 1991

Reproduced by arrangement with
Victor Gollancz Ltd

British Library C.I.P.
Paterson, Katherine
  Star of the night.—(Gold)
  I. Title   II. Series
  823[J]

ISBN 0-340-53135-5

Printed and bound in Great Britain for
Hodder Christian Paperbacks, a
division of Hodder and Stoughton
Ltd, Mill Road, Dunton Green,
Sevenoaks, Kent TN13 2YA (Editorial
Office: 47 Bedford Square, London
WC1B 3DP) by Cox & Wyman Ltd,
Reading.

These stories,
which were first told
in Takoma Park Presbyterian Church,
are for Mary and Raymond Womeldorf,
who first told me the story.

Contents

Angels &
Other Strangers

Minutes after the letter came from Arlene, Jacob set out walking for Washington. He wondered how long it would take him to get there. Before the truck died, he could make it in an hour, but he'd never tried to walk it. At sixty he knew that he didn't have the endurance that he had once had, but he was still a strong man. Perhaps he could get there by morning if he kept a steady pace. Or if he could at least reach a place where there was a bus, he could ride as far as the few bills in his pocket could take him.

Arlene needed him, so he would go to her if he had to walk every step of the way. Arlene, his baby granddaughter, whom it seemed as if he had only just stopped bouncing on his knee, was going to have a baby herself. She was alone and scared in the city and wanted her granddaddy, so he had put on his dead wife's overcoat and then his own and started out. The two coats protected him from the wet snow, but his wife's was too small and cut under his arms. "I'm coming, Arlene baby," he said to the country road. "I'm going to be with you for Christmas."

How wonderful it would be, thought Jacob, if someone stopped and offered him a ride. Occasionally a car would pass, even on this almost deserted stretch. Once he almost raised his arm to try to wave one down, but thought better of it. Who would give a ride to a black man on a lonely road? He could hope in the Lord, but he'd better rely on his own two feet. No rest, as the Good Book said, for the weary.

In Washington, Julia Thompson was humming as she worked. Why was she so happy? Because she had two beautiful children and a loving husband. Because Walter, her husband, would be singing at the Christmas Eve service, and she always felt so proud and was thrilled by his voice. Because it was nearly Christmas. Yes, of course, all those things, but, hallelujah, it was the first Christmas since she'd known Walter that she hadn't had to deal with his Aunt Patty.

Aunt Patty was Walter's only living relative. Some respect was due her for his sake, but nothing ever went quite right with Aunt Patty. The best years were the ones when she had simply grumbled her way through the celebration, taking the edge off everyone else's enjoyment. But the last three years, she'd managed to orchestrate a series of disasters, though how could you blame an old lady for falling down on the church walk just before the Christmas Eve service and having to be rushed to the hospital with a broken hip? Perhaps Aunt Patty should have known enough not to give a two-year-old a teddy bear with button eyes which he could and would immediately pull out and swallow, but she had not known, and it had meant that they had spent Christmas Day with Kevin in the emergency room. Last year, despite Julia's apprehension, everything had gone well, until they, with great excitement, told her the news that they were expecting another child. Aunt Patty, who had never before revealed a social conscience, suddenly burst into a lament for all the starving people in the world. Here they were, gorging themselves and daring to be happy, while at the same time producing still another baby to crowd out the hungry millions.

But this year, despite Walter's urgings, Aunt Patty had decided not to make the thirty-mile trip into the city. The weather was uncertain, and her bursitis had been acting up. Julia cleaned the house and shopped and baked with an energy she hadn't possessed since before Jenny was born. She even had strength left over to take the children on long walks and read aloud to Kevin. It was going to be a wonderful Christmas.

Julia put the baby down for a nap and then took Kevin up on her own bed and began reading to him. Ordinarily, Kevin loved being read to, but today he squirmed and wriggled straight through "The Night Before Christmas."

"My, you're fidgety," she said.

"Little boys are supposed to be fidgety," he said with dignity.

She hugged him close. "Now this is the story from the Bible about when Jesus was born. Try to listen, all right?"

"All right."

She read him the story of Mary and Joseph coming down from Nazareth to Bethlehem, stopping to explain about the taxes, the crowded inn, and the manger, going on to the shepherds in the field.

" 'And, lo, the angel of the Lord came upon them, and the glory of the Lord'—well, it's like a great light, Kevin—'shone round about them: and they were sore afraid. And the angel said unto them, Fear not . . .' "

"Why were they afraid, Mommy?"

"I don't know—I guess the light and the strangeness. They'd never seen a real angel before."

He seemed satisfied. She read on, and since he was beginning to nod, she finished the whole chapter in a quiet voice until he was sound asleep. Julia propped pillows around him and went into the kitchen to clean up the lunch things and get ready for the evening. It was then that she discovered that they had no tangerines. Perhaps she was being silly, Kevin was only four and Jenny scarcely five months, but a Christmas stocking without a tangerine in the toe seemed somehow incomplete, and Julia was determined that this be a perfect Christmas. She got Becky the teen-ager from next door to baby-sit long enough to let her drive to the grocery store to pick up a few. She was home within twenty minutes.

"Everything quiet?" she asked the sitter.

"Sure. Fine. Your aunt called."

Julia's heart sank. "She said to tell you she'd changed her mind and would Mr. Thompson please come pick her up."

Julia should have asked Becky to stay with the children and

gone then and there to get Aunt Patty, but she didn't. She paid Becky a dollar and sent her home before she tried to figure out what to do. Could she pretend she never got the message? No. She dialed Walter's office, looking at her watch as she did so. It was now three thirty. If he could leave Washington right away, he could drive the thirty-odd miles to Bethel, pick up Aunt Patty, and get back in time for his rehearsal. But when his secretary finally answered, it was to say that there had been an accident in the plant in Virginia, and that Walter had gone out to see about it. If he called in, she would have him call home.

That settled it. It was too late. There was no way to get Aunt Patty today, unless— Reluctantly she dialed the neighbors. No, Becky had already gone out with friends. She'd tried, Julia told herself. She really had. No one would expect her to put two sleeping children in the car and drive halfway across Maryland in bad weather.

The phone rang. "Julia?" It was, of course, Aunt Patty. "I want you just to forget my message. You mustn't bother Walter about me at such a busy time. It looks like snow anyhow. It would be ridiculous to come all the way out here."

Kevin came padding down the hall in his sock feet. "Who's that, Mommy?" he asked, still half asleep.

"Aunt Patty," Julia said.

"Aunt Patty!" His face lit up. "She's coming for Christmas!"

"Now I don't want you to feel bad," Aunt Patty was saying. "Just forget all about me and have a wonderful—"

5

"Aunt Patty," Julia broke in wearily, "we'll be there to get you as soon as we can."

There was a silence at the other end of the line. "Well, I think it's ridiculous to try to make it out here in this weather, but. . . . Well, all right. Since you insist."

Julia woke the baby and bundled both children into the car. It was already getting dark and snowing lightly, but she couldn't honestly say that the roads were dangerous. Even driving slowly, she should have plenty of time to get out to Aunt Patty's house in the country and back in time for the service. Of course she hadn't counted on the crowded interstate on Christmas Eve afternoon. They alternately crawled and sat, motors idling, horns honking about them.

On the back seat Jenny slept while Kevin chattered away. He was so excited about getting his Aunt Patty that he sang songs about it, substituting Aunt Patty for Santa Claus. I ought to deserve some credit, Julia thought, that despite everything, I've never turned Kevin against her.

It was nearly five before they were off the main highway and moving at a decent rate of speed. If the visibility had been really poor or the road icy, Julia would have turned around for home even then. But there was no way she could escape this journey now without disappointing her little boy and making herself feel like Scrooge incarnate.

They were dangerously low on gas, but there was a station just this side of Aunt Patty's place where she could fill up, so she pushed on. When they got there, though, the station was closed for the holiday, so she drove on to Aunt Patty's house.

"Just wait with Jenny, Kevin. I'll run in and get Aunt Patty, and we'll be right back." She dashed from the driveway to the back door and banged. It was bitter cold, though the snow was slackening. She tried the door. It fell open. "Aunt Patty?" she called in the hallway. One of Aunt Patty's cats came bouncing down the steps, meowing menacingly. "Aunt Patty?" She was seized with a sudden panic that the old woman might be lying somewhere in the house, ill or worse. Then her eye fell on the note on the kitchen table.

"Walter," it said. "I've just run up to Gertrude's for a minute. You can pick me up there or wait here for me. I won't be long. Love." Walter, were he here, might know who Gertrude was, but Julia had no notion. She wouldn't even know how to look her up in the phone book.

She went back to the car.

"Where's Aunt Patty?" asked Kevin. Where indeed was Aunt Patty?

"She went to see a friend and is coming back soon. We'll go put some gas in the car. By the time we get back, she'll probably be here."

"Why'd she go away? Didn't she know we were coming?"

Julia started the engine and began backing down the drive. She was not going to ruin Christmas by losing her temper.

"Why, Mommy?"

"I don't know, Kevin. She didn't tell me."

"Did you see her?"

"No. She left a note." Addressed to Walter, naturally.

"What did the note say?"

"She just said she was going out for a few minutes and would be right back."

7

"Why?"

"Kevin!"

"Why'd you yell at me, Mommy?"

"Please, Kevin. I've got to watch the road." Where in the world was the nearest gas station? One that would still be open at five thirty on Christmas Eve? There was a housing development with a shopping center somewhere about—she had driven there once with Walter—if she could remember the road to take to cut over to it. Aunt Patty's road was a narrow two-lane country road with very few houses. The windshield wipers pushed the snow aside, and she sat hunched forward, peering out into the path of the headlights, not daring to glance at the gas gauge.

In the darkness, nothing looked familiar. She rarely came out here, and when she did, Walter always drove. She should have stayed and waited for Aunt Patty, but it was too late now to try to turn around and get back.

"Why are you stopping the car, Mommy?"

Julia put her head down on the wheel. She was not going to panic. She had two children to look after. She had to think clearly.

The baby woke up and began to scream.

"The baby woke up, Mommy."

"I know, sweetheart."

"Why'd you stop the car?"

"Don't get upset, Kevin. We've just run out of gas. Everything will be all right. Just don't get upset."

"I'm not upset. The baby's upset. I'm fidgety."

"Well, you can get out of your seat for a while." She

8

reached back and undid his seat belt. He clambered happily into the front seat.

"Oh, tuna fish," he cursed, four-year-old style. "It's stopped snowing."

Julia took Jenny out of the car bed. One thing at a time. First, the baby must be fed. As she nursed the baby, she began to sing to entertain Kevin, who was jealous that his sister could have her supper while he could not.

They were singing about glories streaming from heaven afar when Kevin spotted the light ahead. "Look, Mommy!"

Jacob had first seen the headlights come quickly over a rise far down the road and then as quickly disappear. He kept walking, swinging his huge flashlight as he went, expecting them to reappear at any moment. Not that it mattered. The car was heading the wrong way for him anyhow, even if by some miracle it was someone who would consider giving him a ride. At least it had stopped snowing. Just then the beam of his flashlight caught a car sitting in the darkness. There were people inside. He hesitated a moment. What if it were a trick? For himself he didn't mind dying. Lord knew he was ready to go, but Arlene needed him now. He had to get to Washington. Yet here, perhaps, was somebody else in need. He started across the road, heading for the driver's side of the car.

"Look, Mommy!" Kevin said again. "Glory streams from heaven afar." A strong bright light moved over the rise and

9

down the hill toward them. Julia stopped singing and watched it come. Finally, behind the light, she could make out the tall bulging shadow of a man. She checked quickly to make sure all the doors were locked, took the baby off her breast, and straightened her clothes with a shaking hand. The light was coming straight for her window. Her eyes blinked to shut out the brightness, and when she opened them, a huge black face, which seemed to fill the side window of the small car, was there within inches of her cheek. She pulled back. The man tapped on the window with a worn brown glove that showed the tips of his fingers, and said something through the glass. Julia squeezed the baby tighter and stared straight ahead.

Kevin leaned across her and banged the glass. "Hi!" he said.

"Hi yourself."

Out of the corner of her eye Julia could see the black face smiling broadly. The chin was covered with silver bristles and several teeth were missing. She tried to grab at Kevin to shush him.

"Need some help?" This time the man was shouting as though to make sure she could hear him plainly through the window, but she refused to turn her head.

"Mommy, why don't you answer the nice man?"

"Shh, Kevin. We don't know what he wants."

"He wants to know if we need some help."

The man leaned close to the glass and shouted again. "Don't be afraid, little lady."

"You hear that, Mommy?"

"Kevin, please."

"But, Mommy, he said, 'Don't be afraid!' That's what *angels* say."

"Kevin, no!"

But before she could catch him, Kevin had slid across the seat, pulled up the button, opened the door, and jumped out of the car. The man immediately started around to meet him.

"Don't you touch my child!" Julia screamed, twisting awkwardly from under the wheel, still clutching the baby.

"You don't want him running out into the road, do you, lady?"

"No. No. Thank you." She took Kevin's hand.

"I saw your car and figured you was in trouble."

There was no way to ignore him now. But she had to be careful. He was over six feet tall and obviously strong. The police-pamphlet directions flashed across her brain: *Be sure to look carefully at your assailant so you can give an accurate description to the police later.* If there was a later. Oh, God, don't let him hurt me. Don't let him hurt the children.

"We run out of gas," said Kevin.

Why was she so afraid of him? He, Jacob, who had never willfully hurt the least one of God's creatures—couldn't she tell by looking at him that he only wanted to help? Even the child could see that. He stretched out his hand to put it on the boy's head, but seeing the look in the woman's eyes, he brought it back.

"Your old car's got a empty belly, huh?"

The boy giggled. "Me, too," he said. "I haven't even had my supper."

"Well, we gotta do something about that. I passed a gas station a while back," Jacob said to the woman. "You don't have a can, do you?"

She shook her head. She seemed to be shivering.

"You better get back in the car and try to stay warm." He turned and started back up the hill, sighing as he retraced the descent of a few minutes before. It seemed to have grown steeper. But, at least, praise the Lord, the snow had stopped and the sky was clearing.

"Wait," she called after him. "You'll need some money."

"I got some," Jacob said. He didn't want to waste time and energy going back down the hill.

Suppose he never came back? Would they grow cold and sleepy and freeze out here in the middle of nowhere on Christmas Eve? Well, Aunt Patty, you will have certainly beaten your own record this year—even Christmas morning in the emergency room will pale in comparison. And then suppose he did come back? What did he want? He could have just taken her purse and run, if money was what he wanted. But of course it was the car he was after, so he could get away faster —but she tried not to think of that.

"I think we should sing some more songs," Kevin said. "I might forget about my tummy."

Julia was glad for the diversion. They sang through every carol she knew, even la-la-ing through unfamiliar verses. Then they sang all the songs on Kevin's favorite records, then another round of Christmas carols. Until at long last they saw the light coming over the hill.

"Here comes the glory light," said Kevin.

This time when the man came to her window, she rolled it down. "Would you hold the flashlight for me while I pour the gas in?" he asked.

Trembling, she laid Jenny down in the car bed and went around to the tank. He handed her his big torch, which she tried to hold steady as he poured.

"Well, thank you," Julia said when he had finished, keeping her voice cool. "Let me pay you something for all your trouble."

Jacob looked at her. She was going to give him some money and drive off. He had given her nearly an hour of his time and far more of his energy than he could spare. There was no way she could pay him for that. But she had already gone to the front seat and gotten her purse, the little boy scampering around her at every step.

"That's all right," he said. "Forget it."

She stuck a few bills out at him. "But I owe you for the gas."

"I—uh—do need to return the can. If you could give me a ride down the road and back. . . ."

She nodded.

He could tell by her eyes that she didn't want him in her car, but, Lord, she owed him that much. He decided to ignore her eyes.

"Well, old man," he said to the child, "let's see if we can get this old buggy going." He took the boy around and put him in his seat, letting the child tell him how to buckle the belt, and then climbed into the front seat.

The woman put her purse down between them and buckled herself in. Jacob looked down at the purse and then realized she had caught him looking. He quickly shifted his gaze. "Just down the road a couple miles or so," he said.

Within ten minutes they were at the lighted station. She gave the can back to the attendant and asked him to fill the tank. She saw his eyes question the presence of the man on the seat beside her. Should she try to signal for help? It seemed too foolish. The man had done nothing except try to help her —so far. She at least owed him a ride home on this freezing night.

"We come to get my Aunt Patty to take her home for Christmas." Oh, Kevin.

"Is that a fact? Where's your home, old man?"

Don't answer him, Kevin. But of course Kevin, who had memorized his full address at nursery school, recited it in a proud singsong: "Thirteen-oh-six Essex Street Northwest, Washington, D. C. Two-oh-oh-one-six."

"My, you're one smart boy."

"I know," said Kevin.

❄   ❄   ❄

I could get a ride all the way to Washington tonight, Jacob said to himself. All I have to do is ask. But he couldn't make himself say the words. If the woman had seemed in the least bit friendly, the least bit trusting, he would have asked her. But how could he ask a favor of a person who thought he was going to grab her purse or hurt her kids?

She had started the car and was pulling out of the station. "Where shall I let you off?" she asked.

It was his chance to tell her. She owed him something, didn't she? And Arlene was waiting, not even knowing if he had gotten her letter.

"Just down the road," he mumbled. "Just anywhere."

They drove past the place where they had met, but he gave no sign of wanting to be let out, so Julia drove on. She couldn't just stop in the middle of nowhere and order him out. What should she do? They went on until she could see Aunt Patty's house ablaze with light. Aunt Patty was home. Thank God for small blessings.

"Here's where my Aunt Patty lives," Kevin told the stranger.

"Is that a fact?"

The problem of how to get Aunt Patty without leaving the children alone in the car with the man solved itself. Aunt Patty came rushing out of the house, coat and suitcase flying. She had obviously been watching for the car. When she saw Julia at the wheel, she was furious. "Where have you been?" she demanded. "You're going to make me miss the music."

Julia opened her mouth to defend herself, but at the same moment her passenger got out of the car. He stood there tall and straight against the starry winter sky.

"Mercy!" Aunt Patty screamed. "What in the world?"

"He's our angel, Aunt Patty. Our Christmas angel."

"Don't be ridiculous, Kevin."

Ridiculous indeed! All Julia's fears evaporated in a puff of anger. How dare Aunt Patty call it ridiculous? The man had been an angel. She leaned across the seat and called out, "Would you mind squeezing in back with the children?"

Even in the darkness she thought she could see him smile.

"Get in, Aunt Patty," she commanded, "or you'll make us miss the music."

A little farther down the road she turned to him. "How far can I take you?"

"I need to go all the way to Washington," he said.

"Oh, goody!" cried Kevin. "Then you can go to church with us! We never had a real angel in our church before."

He patted the boy's knee. "Can't make it this time, old man," he said. "I got to go see this lonesome little girl. Cheer her up for Christmas."

"Angels are really busy, aren't they?"

Jacob laughed, a great rich sound which filled the car. "Yeah," he said. "We keep busy, but it's mighty pleasant work."

Aunt Patty may have said something that sounded like "ridiculous," but Julia joyfully chose to ignore it. This was going to be a perfect Christmas.

Guests

Whenever Pastor Nagai thought of his wife, he remembered the day last summer when she had taken her silk wedding kimono from the trunk and sold it for two tomatoes. The children had been so hungry. But the children were not hungry now. They would never be hungry again—nor full nor sad nor happy—nor alive.

With a crash of fire the tiny house had exploded, and they were all gone—his wife, his son, and the baby girl. One of her tiny sandals had been found in front of the greengrocer's nearly two blocks away.

Even as he had tried to fight his way into the burning wreckage of his home, he had heard a voice cry out: "Oh, pastor, where is your foreign god that he did not protect you from the American bombers? Is he asleep?"

"Perhaps"—another voice had joined the jeering—"he thinks all Japanese look alike!"

His heart's pain had soon blocked out the sound of the laughter. A few years before, these people who had been his neighbors had smiled and bowed politely to him on the street. Now he had become their enemy, a traitor to his native land, because he preached of the Americans' god. So great was their hatred that even the death of his family failed to draw from them a drop of human compassion.

His friend Pastor Tanaka had bicycled the twenty miles from Kawajima to hold the service at which Pastor Nagai was the only mourner. One could hardly count the policeman who had stood at the back with his arms crossed until Tanaka had mentioned "the Kingdom of God," at which he had whipped a small notebook from his pocket and proceeded to take notes.

Pastor Nagai was so alone. For a while he had tried to keep on having Sunday services. For two years they had been held at midnight and in secret so that the police would not harass the little congregation, for at first a few believers had continued to come. But, one by one, they had dropped away until only he and his wife and the sleeping children were there for the whispered hymns and prayers.

Now only he was left. He tried to pray a little each day and to read the scriptures, but he found himself turning again and again to the Psalms of anguish:

> *I am stricken, withered like grass*
> *I cannot find the strength to eat.*
> *Wasted away, I groan aloud*
> *And my skin hangs on my bones. . . .*
> *My enemies insult me all the day long;*

Mad with rage they conspire against me.
I have eaten ashes for bread
And mingled tears with my drink.
  In thy wrath and fury
    thou hast taken me and flung me aside. . . .
My God, my God, why hast thou forsaken me?

Winter came, and nothing changed except the weather, which was cruel. He had moved into a corner of the tiny sanctuary, since the house had been destroyed, and there with whatever rags he could find stuffed about the windows, he tried to keep from freezing, huddled over a smoky charcoal burner. People died from such fumes, he knew—and sometimes hoped.

And then suddenly one day it was Christmas Eve. He had not remembered it, but, passing a shop window, he had seen a calendar with a large 24 printed in bright pink. His first thought was of his dead children, who had never known a Christmas without war. And then he thought of the year before, when his wife had tried so hard to find a merchant who would sell her a little rice for their Christmas dinner. She had had a silk brocade sash, which had been in her family for three generations, that she would gladly have traded for a cup, even half a cup of rice, but the police had warned the merchants not to sell food to the traitors of Japan, so she had come home empty-handed.

Afterward, he himself had walked five miles into the country, which is a long journey on an empty stomach, to see a farmer who was a Christian and whose son the pastor had once helped prepare for his university entrance exams. The kind man had shared the last of his own grain, refusing to accept the sash in exchange. "You'll need it another day," he said.

How happy they had been last Christmas! Real rice, and almost enough of it to stop the constant pains in their empty bellies.

As he boiled the roots that were to be his meager meal, the memories of last Christmas, the farmer's generosity, and his family's joy shook loose the tentacles of his self-pity. From the closet he scrounged the stubs of some ancient Christmas candles. He would light them and have a proper service. To the devil with the police!

That afternoon he planned the hymns, even wrote a sermon, as though he were expecting fifty people to crowd into the little church, when, in fact, he expected no one at all. But it would be a proper service, and maybe his wife in heaven would know that he remembered her and for her sake had tried to worship the Infant King.

At ten he lit his seven stubby candles and seated himself at the wheezing pump organ.

> *Joy to the world! the Lord is come:*
> *Let earth receive her King. . . .*

He sang at the top of his voice, daring that slick-booted young policeman who had burned up his volumes of Karl Barth to march in and arrest him. He almost prayed for the man to come. Why should he care if he were thrown into jail? What was this building, this town, to him but a jail?

Guests

Let every heart prepare him room,
And heaven and nature sing.

He sang through all the verses and was tempted to repeat them, but as this was to be a proper service, he slid off the organ bench and stood behind the wooden pulpit. He bowed his head and closed his eyes.

"Let us pray."

"Oh, don't stop the music!"

The pastor's eyes popped open. In the doorway stood a little girl. About seven, he guessed, though he was seldom able to guess accurately, since his son had been only three when he died. Even in the dim candlelight he could see that she was dressed in rags, and he recognized her as a Korean child. The government had brought over laborers from Korea a few years before and impressed into service for the war effort. They were housed in shacks on the other side of town.

"Would you like to come in for the meeting?" he asked gently.

She nodded, and slipping off her straw sandals, she climbed up into the room, her hands behind her back. She slid onto the floor before him and looked up expectantly.

He went on with the prayer, but he made it a short one. Children wiggled so terribly during long prayers, he remembered.

He inserted several more carols than he had planned, because the congregation obviously enjoyed the music most of all, and he skipped the offering entirely as most probably unnecessary.

Then there was the sermon. The careful notes, based on Jeremiah and on his memory of Karl Barth, were tucked into the back of his hymn book. He leaned over the pulpit and looked into the child's face. Her eyes were shining in the candlelight, as was her nose. Did all the children whom Jesus took on his knee have runny noses? He was tempted to offer her his handkerchief, ragged as it was, but he was afraid to offend her.

"Do you know about Jesus?"

She shook her head.

"Do you know, then, that there is one God who made the world and all of us in it?"

She shook her head again. And so the pastor began with Genesis and told her the story of God and man until he came to the time when God became man at Bethlehem.

"In a cave?" she asked. "Just like the cave we hide in when the bombers come?"

"Yes," he replied, "except there were no bombers then. They used the cave as a house for farm animals. Like a barn."

But she had never seen a barn. "If there were no bombers, was there no war in that country?"

"No war. That was over, but the great empire of Rome had won the war and conquered the tiny country, so there were many soldiers about."

"And secret police who beat you when you speak Korean in front of them?"

"Yes, secret police, I'm sure."

"And what did the new king do? Did he kill all the wicked soldiers and police?"

"No, he wasn't that kind of king."

The child was puzzled. Kings and emperors and presidents had power to crush and destroy in the world she knew. Surely a king . . . ?

"No. He went about helping people. If they were sick, he made them well."

"Did he give them money and food?"

"Sometimes food. He didn't have any money."

"Then what happened?"

"He died. That is, he was killed. The soldiers and leaders and a lot of the people hated him, and they had him killed."

"Why should they hate him?"

"I'm not completely sure. Perhaps they were afraid of his goodness. Perhaps they thought he was a traitor. Or perhaps they resented the way he loved the poor and the unhappy people."

"Did he love Koreans and Christ lovers, too?"

"Yes." The pastor smiled. "Even those."

"Is that all the story?"

"Oh, no. If that were the end of the story, we would be hopeless. Our King would be dead." And as the pastor told of how the King had died and then risen, some light dawned in his own dark spirit. "He is alive. Right here with us. But we can't see him."

"Yes, we can," the child said. "You look like the king." She got up and padded barefoot to him, and as she did so, she took her hand from behind her back and held out to him a roasted sweet potato. How had he missed the smell earlier? It came to his nostrils now like the sweet manna of the wilderness. The

23

two of them sat down together while he carefully divided the treasure—she must have stolen it—and ate it slowly together.

He hated for the evening to end, but he knew it must be very late. The night watchman calling the hour before midnight had passed by some time ago. At first she protested, but at last consented to go when he promised more music and stories another day.

He bade her good night and began to extinguish the candles, which were now nothing but wicks swimming in puddles of wax.

"Uncle."

He looked up to see the child in the doorway. And behind her, standing half-hidden in the shadows, was the figure of a man. He knew without seeing the face that it was the shiny-booted policeman who had confiscated his bicycle, burned his books, and taken notes at his wife's funeral. A thrill of fear went through him. How long had the policeman been standing there? What had he heard? Lord, what had he said in that crazy sermon? But he did not want the child to see his fear, so he said simply: "Come back in, little one, and bring your friend in with you."

"I found him waiting outside the door," she explained.

"Perhaps he liked the music, too."

The policeman stepped up into the church without bothering to remove his boots. The pastor pretended not to notice. "My son," he said, "the service was just ending, but since you've taken such trouble to come, perhaps you would like for us to continue it a little longer?"

The younger man's lips curled for a sarcastic reply, but the pastor did not wait for it.

"If you'll just sit there in the front with the child. . . . " He looked straight into the proud face. To Pastor Nagai's surprise he found it to be a young face. The eyes above the sneering mouth shifted slightly under the pastor's gaze. It is only a child, the pastor realized, another child who has never heard the story.

He took his place behind the pulpit and opened the Bible. There was only moonlight now, too dark for him to read by, but he knew the passage by heart.

"And it came to pass in those days there went out a decree from Caesar Augustus that all the world should be taxed. . . ." The policeman took out a notebook and began to write.

"And, lo, the angel of the Lord came upon them, and the glory of the Lord shone round about them: and they were sore afraid. And the angel said unto them, Fear not. . . ." For the first time in many years, Pastor Nagai obeyed the angel's word.

Many
Happy Reruns

Elizabeth wished Miss Violet would stop singing. She had a screechy voice that hurt Elizabeth's ears like the *wheee* when her mother would let the teakettle stay on too long. The song had gone on too long. Sunday School had gone on too long. And Miss Violet had gone on far too long. Elizabeth felt like saying "Shut up" just like that, right in the middle of the class. Wouldn't everybody be surprised if she did that? Just "Shut up." She said it over again inside her head. Why couldn't kids say "Shut up" to grown-ups? Grown-ups were always saying it to children. Maybe not "Shut up," but "Will you *please* be quiet while your mother is trying to rest?"

"Has everyone seen the manger scene in the big church?" Miss Violet had finally stopped singing and started teaching.

"Ye-es," said all the children except Elizabeth, who was studying the crack in the wall above Miss Violet's head. If you took a crayon and put a thing with two points at the round part, it would look just like a snake getting ready to bite.

"And who remembers why Jesus was born?"

"To save us from our sins!" All the children yelled except Elizabeth.

"Elizabeth"—Miss Violet leaned over the picture she was holding of Baby Jesus in the manger—"Elizabeth, we're talking about something very important to all of us. Don't you want Jesus to save you from your sins?"

"Yes'm." Except that Elizabeth was extremely fuzzy on just what sins she wished to be saved from. Was punching Willis Morgan in the stomach when he called you a dumdum a sin? She hardly thought so. Even God must know you couldn't help that. Was it a sin to wish that stupid baby would hurry up and be born so Aunt Gladys would go away and never come back again? How could it be? Was it a sin to hate Aunt Gladys? Probably. But it wasn't a sin she wanted to be saved from. No—sin was like killing somebody when you weren't even a policeman or a cowboy—like hating somebody for no reason.

She didn't hate Miss Violet. She didn't feel much of anything toward Miss Violet. Except for her singing, which was terrible, the rest of Miss Violet was all right. She was kind of like the church—very old and crumbly, mostly boring but not scary. It was probably because Miss Violet had always lived right next door to the church ever since she was Elizabeth's age and her father was the minister. He had died many years before Elizabeth was born. Most of the old houses on the block had long ago been bulldozed for stores or apartments, but Miss Violet wouldn't sell "dear Poppa's manse."

Elizabeth sighed. Her best friend Kimberly Wood stayed

home all Sunday morning and watched TV. They had old movies and *Wonderama* with cartoons, Kimberly said. Why didn't Elizabeth's mother or father come and pick her up? Church was like a rerun of a dumb show you didn't like the first time, but at least there Elizabeth could sit squeezed between her parents and draw pictures on the backs of the pew envelopes. It was crazy. If you sat for the hour drawing on the backs of the envelopes, everyone would tell your parents afterward what a wonderful little girl they had and weren't they proud. But if you tried to listen to all the preaching and praying and when you didn't understand something, just whisper a tiny little question, both your parents looked angry and said "Shh!" and nobody said how good you were.

Elizabeth sighed again. Why didn't her mother and father pick her up?

But, of course, today her mother wouldn't come and get her. Her mother was in the hospital having that stupid baby. When Elizabeth had waked up this morning, neither her father nor her mother had been in their bed. There was just Aunt Gladys, grinning and clucking about. But she didn't grin when Elizabeth picked up her whole sunny-side egg with her fingers and ate it in one gulp. No, she didn't grin then, she yelped like Scooby Do when he saw a ghost. Elizabeth had to giggle when she remembered it.

Aunt Gladys was standing at the Sunday School door, waiting for Miss Violet to finish her prayer. She was staring right at Elizabeth. What could she have done wrong now? She hadn't seen Aunt Gladys for an hour.

"Elizabeth, you should bow your head and close your eyes

during the prayer," Aunt Gladys said as she helped Elizabeth put on her coat. "Don't you know God wants us to worship him reverently?"

It occurred to Elizabeth that Aunt Gladys must also have forgotten to close her eyes during the prayer, and she was sorely tempted to say so, but "Yes'm" was all she actually said.

"We can't stay for church this morning," Aunt Gladys said as she took Elizabeth's hand. "Your father may be trying to reach us." After they crossed the first street, Elizabeth slipped her hand away and into her pocket and kept it there for the six long cold blocks to the tall skinny house where Elizabeth lived.

There wasn't even a decoration on the door. Elizabeth had seen a huge Santa Claus in the dime store last week, but she couldn't persuade Aunt Gladys to buy it. Santa Claus probably wouldn't come this year. When she'd told her mother she wanted a "Baby Alive" just as they advertised on TV, her mother had laughed and said, "Oh, we'll have a baby alive all right. That will be enough diapers for this Christmas." So when her father had asked her if she'd rather have a baby brother or a baby sister for Christmas, she'd said right out, "I'd rather have a two-wheeler with a banana seat." He'd laughed as though he thought she was kidding, but she wasn't kidding a bit. She didn't want some dumb baby for a Christmas present. They'd probably stop having Christmas ever again. Every year it would be the baby's birthday, and they'd all be so busy buying it presents and making it a cake that they wouldn't even remember to have Christmas.

The phone was ringing when they opened the door. Elizabeth ran through the hall as fast as she could to get there first, but Aunt Gladys took the receiver right out of her hand.

"Ohhh, Richard, that's *lovely.* Now isn't that just the right weight? A perfect baby." Elizabeth was jumping up and down. She thought she would scream if Aunt Gladys didn't shut up and give her the phone back. "And how is Linda? . . . Well, that's quite natural. I know you're thrilled . . . What's the name, now?"

Elizabeth couldn't keep still any longer. "Give it to me! Give it to me! I gotta talk to Daddy."

But Aunt Gladys acted as though she didn't hear. She began to give Elizabeth's father a long list of relatives that he ought to call right away.

"Give it to me!" Elizabeth begged.

Aunt Gladys put her hand over the mouth of the receiver. "Be quiet for one minute, please, Elizabeth. Oh, I think that's a mistake, Richard. You said yourself she was worn out. You tell her to take it easy and take all the time she needs to build up her strength. We'll do just fine here. . . ."

Elizabeth went up the stairs to her room. The bed with the pink spread was really hers, but now Aunt Gladys was sleeping in it and Elizabeth had to use the cot. She plopped down on the cot. Never before in her life had she been so angry that she couldn't even cry. She picked up Ernie and punched him hard in the stomach. He smiled his shoe-button smile. There was a hole behind his ear, and some of his stuffing was coming out. She tried to push it back in, but it crumbled up in her hand. "Shut up," she said to Ernie, but he just kept on smiling. She stuck her fingers into the hole and tore it a little more. It tore neatly with a rip-rip-rip kind of sound, so she kept on tearing.

The first thing Aunt Gladys said to her father when he came home that evening was that Elizabeth had "maliciously destroyed" her toy dog and strewn the stuffings all over the bed. Elizabeth wasn't familiar with the word "maliciously," but it sounded as though it ought not to rhyme with "deliciously." Her father looked hurt and disappointed and tired, which made Elizabeth sorry. Perhaps it was a sin to kill a stuffed dog. At any rate she felt bad, looking at him in the wastebasket, his smile still sewed onto a funny flat face.

But her father was not angry. He sat in his big brown chair and pulled Elizabeth up into his lap. She snuggled up under his chin, which was all prickly.

"You tickle, Daddy."

"No time to shave this morning, Snicklefritz." He rubbed his chin hard against her cheek to tease her. Elizabeth giggled. "Did Aunt Gladys tell you about your new brother?"

Elizabeth shook her head. Of course, Aunt Gladys had, but she wanted to hear it from her daddy. She sighed happily as he began to tell her the story of how he and Mommy had rushed out that morning when the whole city was still asleep . . . Oh, yes, of course the firemen and policemen and doctors and nurses and the people at the TV station were awake.

"How about Jesus?"

"No, Jesus wasn't asleep. He was watching over you and Mommy and the baby about to be born."

"And you, too?"

"Me, too, Snicklefritz."

Though why anyone as big as Daddy needed Jesus to look after him was more than Elizabeth could understand.

Her father went on with the story—how Baby Joshua came yelling into the world—and how he and Mommy decided to call him Joshua out of the Bible because it means "God is deliverance," which is the same thing that "Jesus" means and Joshua and Jesus would have almost the same birthday.

And then he told her that Joshua weighed seven pounds, eight ounces . . . but why was that important? The important thing was that her mother was going to come home on Christmas Eve—"Yes, Gladys, the doctor is sure it's all right"—so they would all be together for Christmas.

Elizabeth could have died of joy on the spot. Her mother coming home—Aunt Gladys would go away, and then the three of them could be happy again just as they used to be.

On Christmas Eve, Elizabeth's mother came as her father had promised, but it was not the same. In the first place, Aunt Gladys did not leave. And in the second place, everyone was always kitchy-cooing over this baby.

Elizabeth could hardly stand it. He wasn't even cute. He was bald, and his face was the color of a cherry cough drop when he cried—which was most of the time. Her mother let her sit in the brown chair and hold him, but Joshua screamed right in her face, and Elizabeth knew he hated her even if she was his sister. She didn't want to hold him anymore. He cried too much. She turned on the TV set, but she could still hear him.

"Maybe he's not getting enough milk!" Aunt Gladys would rush out to fix a bottle, and then she and Elizabeth's mother would have a fight because Elizabeth's mother wanted to feed him all by herself. "And for goodness sake, Gladys, the doctor said to hold off on formula. *Please* I do know what I'm doing."

Grown-ups might call it a disagreement, but Elizabeth could recognize a fight when she heard one. It made her stomach knot up to see her mother angry but still trying to be nice. There was nothing to do but sit around and listen to the grown-ups fuss and hear the baby cry. She didn't want to watch TV. She wanted to decorate the Christmas tree, but her mother said, "Wait for Daddy, please, sweetie," and Elizabeth didn't want to ask Aunt Gladys to help. Then she had a marvelous idea. She'd do it all by herself and surprise everyone. All anyone had said lately was what a big girl she had to be now that there was to be a new baby around. "I'm sure you're going to be a real helper for your mother." That's what Miss Violet had said on Sunday.

She even knew where in the attic the Christmas box was kept. It was too heavy for her, but that was all right. She could carry a few things down at a time. On the first trip she carried the lights and one box of balls. The balls were tricky. She had to keep sliding them back so they wouldn't fall off the top of the pile, but she managed. Proudly she set the load down under the tree and went back for more.

She passed her mother carrying Joshua in the upstairs hall. "What are you doing, sweetie?" she asked, but Elizabeth could see that her eyes were looking that funny way that meant she wasn't really paying attention. "Nothing," Elizabeth answered, and her mother smiled and said, "Fine." Then her mother carried Joshua to the little room Daddy had fixed up and put him back to bed. When she came out again, she smiled vaguely at Elizabeth and went into her own room and lay down. Good. She'd go to sleep, and when she woke up, Elizabeth would have the tree all beautiful for her.

The last load was the heaviest. Elizabeth started to divide it and come back for the manger scene, but it was a long trip, and she was in a hurry, so she put the shoe box with the manger scene on top of everything else and started slowly down the two flights of stairs to the living room. She was almost to the landing. . . . Careful, careful, just a little farther.

"Elizabeth. What are you doing?"

Elizabeth jerked upright, and the shoe box slid off, turned in the air, and crashed at the bottom of the stairs.

"Oh, no!" Aunt Gladys cried. Then she fell to her knees and unwrapped the tissue paper, revealing a shattered shepherd. "It's the porcelain Nativity that my father brought from Germany before I was born. I've loved it ever since I was a tiny child. And now—now—"

Elizabeth didn't know what to do. She just stood there with her arms full of boxes of balls and tinsel. She hoped the Baby Jesus wasn't broken. She loved the way its eyes were closed with little tiny painted lashes. Jesus did *too* sleep.

"Can't you even say you're sorry? Do you know what you've done?" Aunt Gladys started up the stairs toward Elizabeth.

Elizabeth was scared. She didn't want Aunt Gladys to get her. She threw down the rest of the boxes as hard as she could and ran up the stairs. Her mother was standing at the railing, blocking the way to Elizabeth's own room, so she ran to the baby's room, slammed the door, and leaned against it. The button was right there in the lock on the inside, so she punched it in. Just in time, too, because they were both there, her mother and Aunt Gladys, banging on the door and yelling at her to let them in.

"We've got to get in there, Linda. There's no telling what she might do. The child might do something malicious."

"Gladys!"

"I mean it, Linda. You should have seen the expression on her face when she threw those boxes at me."

"Elizabeth, sweetie, let Mommy in."

"Let us in, Elizabeth. Right this minute!"

The baby began to scream. "Shut up!" yelled Elizabeth. "Shut up." It seemed to her that the baby was yelling even louder.

"What is she doing to the baby? Linda, you've got to get someone—the fire department—the police—someone! She might hurt him."

"Nonsense, Gladys. Elizabeth . . ."

Elizabeth went over to the crib. Joshua's face was all red and all mouth. "Shut up," she said quietly, but she meant it. "If you don't shut up this minute, I'm going to smack you to kingdom come."

"Well, if you won't call someone, I will."

"Joshua, if you don't shut up, Aunt Gladys will call the police, and I'll be in jail for Christmas." Elizabeth was desperate. "Shut up, Joshua. I mean it. Shut up this minute."

"I'm going to call, Linda. Right this minute . . ."

"Gladys, *please* . . ."

Elizabeth lifted her hand over the baby and smacked hard,

35

really hard. Harder than she'd ever punched Willis Morgan, harder than she'd ever hit anybody in the world. For a moment there was dead silence.

I killed him, thought Elizabeth, I killed my own brother. She raced to the window, unlocked it, then shoved it up—just as Daddy had shown her at the fire drill. She threw out the rope fire escape and climbed to the ground. It didn't even matter that she only had a sweater on; she was running too hard to notice. She had to get hold of Jesus at once. If you got put in jail for locking a door, what happened if you killed your own brother? She ran as fast as she could, and when she got to the church door, she yanked on the big handle with all her might. It was locked.

"Jesus," Elizabeth yelled. "Let me in. You gotta help me." She began beating on the door with both her fists. Her teeth were rattling in her head. "Jesus, please, please! You gotta help me."

"Elizabeth?" It was Miss Violet. She had on an old purple sweater, and the front part of her hair was in paper curlers. "Elizabeth, what in the world are you doing here?" Elizabeth threw her arms around the wrinkled old neck. "Oh, Miss Violet! You gotta help me find Jesus. You gotta help me."

Miss Violet took Elizabeth's hand and led her to her own house, where the door stood open. "You scared me out of my wits with all that crying. What are you doing here, anyway, all by yourself with no coat on, even?"

"I killed baby Joshua, Miss Violet. I didn't mean to, but he wouldn't stop screaming and they were going to take me to

36

jail. You gotta tell Jesus to help me. He won't listen to me now. He hates me."

"There, there, just a minute." Miss Violet sat down in her old rocker—the one that had once been "Poppa's chair"—and pulled the sobbing Elizabeth into her lap. "Why don't you tell me what happened." So Elizabeth told her, and Miss Violet didn't interrupt; she didn't fuss; she didn't smile. She just stroked Elizabeth's hair and rocked.

"So what do you want Jesus to do, Elizabeth?" she asked when Elizabeth had finished all the crying she was able to do.

There was a long silence. "He can't make the baby alive again, can he?"

"I gave up a long time ago weighing what he could or couldn't do, Elizabeth."

"That's the main thing." Elizabeth twisted her finger in a hole in Miss Violet's sweater.

"Is that all?"

"He can't save me, can he?"

"What do you mean, Elizabeth?"

"I'm—I'm malicious. That means nobody could save me from my sins."

Miss Violet tightened her arms about Elizabeth. She smelled like the sachet in Mommy's sweater drawer. Her chin was all soft, not prickly like Daddy's. Elizabeth began to cry once more. She would never be able to sit on her father's lap and be called Snicklefritz again.

"Go to Hell." That's what Jesus would say, and her daddy would look sad and tired, but he wouldn't be able to help her.

The tall black gates yawned open before her. Daddy might even hate her, too. Just like Jesus did for killing her little brother. And her mother? Her mother would be so lonely with no more children in the world. . . .

Suddenly Elizabeth sat up and looked hard at Miss Violet. "Why are *you* crying, Miss Violet? You didn't do anything bad."

"Because"—Miss Violet's voice was pinched and tiny— "because I love you very much."

Elizabeth snuffled loudly, and then she sat quietly listening to the creak-creak-creak of Poppa's rocker and Miss Violet's sniffles. Elizabeth couldn't remember ever having seen a grown-up cry before—sometimes on TV but never really and truly. And Miss Violet hadn't done *anything* bad. . . . A tiny light began to grow in her, deep down inside.

"Does Jesus ever cry, Miss Violet?"

"Yes." Miss Violet retrieved a lace-edged handkerchief from her sweater pocket and dabbed her eyes and nose. "Yes, it says so in the Bible. It says, 'Jesus wept.' "

"That's in the Bible?"

Miss Violet nodded.

"Good," said Elizabeth, feeling the light grow inside her, and hearing finally, to her great joy, the black iron gates clang shut. "That is really good to know."

When Aunt Gladys appeared at Miss Violet's door, her face was red and puffy as if she, too, had been crying.

She dropped to her knees and put her arms around Elizabeth. "Oh, you crazy child, you had us frantic." Then she seemed to remember where she was and stood up and thanked Miss Violet. "You can't imagine how I felt. I was terrified. Linda finally got into the room with a screwdriver. There was the baby, screaming his little head off, and nothing left of Elizabeth except an open second-story window. It's a mercy she didn't kill herself climbing out. We couldn't imagine where she'd gone—no coat as you see." Aunt Gladys patted the coat she had brought along. "It was getting dark. We couldn't reach her father." Aunt Gladys blew her nose. "What a relief to get your call. You can't imagine. . . . Her poor mother was panicked, and I—I—it was all my fault. I'm just too old. I just don't know how to deal with children anymore. I wanted to help. I really thought I could help, but it would have been far better if I had never c—"

"Aunt Gladys. Will you *please* be quiet for one minute?" Elizabeth stuck her arms up, and Aunt Gladys, her mouth still open, helped her put on her coat. Then Elizabeth took Aunt Gladys's hand. "We gotta go home now, Miss Violet. Tell Jesus thank you, and happy birthday."

"You tell him yourself, Elizabeth. He's listening."

Elizabeth grinned. "Happy birthday, Jesus," she said softly. "And many happy reruns of the day."

Tidings of Joy

Three months before the baby was born, Carol had a dream. It was one of those dreams pregnant women have that they never tell anyone about, for they are half afraid they will be laughed at—and half afraid the dream might in some terrible way come true. Even the most rational, the least superstitious, women have these irrational fears for their unborn children. And Carol was a rational woman, but she awoke in a cold sweat and was not able to shake the mood of the dream for several days.

In the dream the baby had been born, and she was lying in a very white hospital room, waiting for the nurse to bring the baby in. They had told her it was a girl. She should have felt thrilled. Even when Mark was born, she had wanted a girl and she still felt guilty when she remembered her disappointment. But in the dream, the baby had been a girl. They would call her Joy. Bert and she had kept the name since before Mark's birth. She should have been full of happiness. Yet somehow in the brightness of the dream she was disturbed. She wanted to keep the nurse from coming into the room and showing her the baby. But the nurse in gleaming starched uniform came in and put the baby in her arms. The blanket was covering the infant's face. Carol reached up to uncover the face, and in the dream her arm was leaden.

"Go on," the nurse had said. "Go on. Look at it."

With the chilling dread of the nightmare, Carol had lifted the edge of the blanket and looked down at the baby's face. A huge domed forehead narrowed into a sharp point of a chin. The nose was wide and sunk deeply into the cheeks. Under the eyes were great dark circles, and the eyes themselves—she still shuddered to remember them—were huge and old and empty.

"Serves you right," the nurse had said. "Serves you right."

The dream was too horrible to share, even with Bert. But she wrestled with it inside herself, recognizing the face of the nightmare child as a photo she had seen in a magazine several weeks before—a photo showing bloated-bellied Biafran children. Her subconscious had transferred one of those staring faces to the face of the child she was expecting. Very normal —a completely understandable occurrence. But knowledge did not exorcise the specter as it should have. The eyes continued to haunt her, and into her delighted anticipation, fear poked an icy finger, until at last all her pleasure was gripped with a frozen terror. And she could not share it with anyone.

So when the baby actually came, she had known it was dead before anyone could gently break the news. The doctor had pulled out scientific language to cover his own distress and was explaining the statistical improbability of the event. Her whole pregnancy had proceeded so normally. There had been no warning. . . .

"But it did happen," Bert said, his patient voice full of pain.

"Yes, but . . ."

Serves you right. The words were as clear as though someone in the room had spoken them aloud to her. Carol turned her head to the wall.

Bert managed to get the doctor out of the room. "Do you want to see her?" he asked gently when he came back.

Carol shook her head. How could she bear to see this child whom, despite the statistical improbabilities, she had somehow caused to die.

Later, she had asked Bert if the baby's eyes had been open.

He had looked at her strangely. "No, of course not." But he had stopped himself, not asking the reason for her question, sensing the unreasonableness of it.

Everyone was very kind. Her mother came as originally planned. No one spoke about the baby except Mark, who, being only three, hadn't learned the subtle cruelties of tact.

"But why did the baby die?" Why does the rain fall? Why do I have to go to bed? Why do my fingers wrinkle in the water? For Mark it was only another why. One of the many that Carol had no answer for. She tried to ignore the question. But Mark was insistent. *"Why?"*

"Because," Carol's mother said gently, "God wanted to have Baby Joy in heaven with him."

"No, Mother, don't say that!" Carol said, nearly screaming. She saw her mother shrink.

"I'm sorry, darling. The child needs some answer."

Carol turned away. Why? She was asking inside her head. Why should he have an answer? None of the rest of us do. He's got to learn there are no answers.

Serves you right. That's not an answer! What have I done?

"Oh, my poor baby," her mother was saying, not to Mark but to her. Carol let her mother put her arm around her and take her to bed.

Physically, she grew stronger. Her mother went back to Ohio. The leaves fell, and winter came. Time heals, everyone said. But everyone was wrong. Carol did not heal.

Life must go on, everyone said. And so for their sakes, she went through the motions of living. She got through the annual reunion with Bert's family without embarrassing anyone, despite the fact that her sister-in-law was radiantly pregnant, and Mark was as eager as he had been last spring to feel the baby move.

"Our baby got dead," he said solemnly. There was a painful silence, but even then Carol managed to keep her features composed.

The skin had healed over the place. It was only underneath that the wound was still raw.

And now it was nearly Christmas—the Christmas when they were to have had a baby. A six-month-old daughter bouncing in the jump seat, reaching for the lights. But Christmas would come even without Joy—she paused over the irony of the pun. Life must go on, she reminded herself grimly as she tied Mark's shoes, struggled to put last year's boots over them, and hunted until she found two mittens. They didn't match, but Mark wouldn't care.

She had meant to leave him at the neighbor's while she shopped, but he cried piteously at the thought of being left, and she didn't have the energy to fight him. She was wrong, of course. He was, as she had known he would be, a terrible nuisance everywhere she went. In the dime store he grabbed up a box of Christmas-tree balls, and when she tried to take them from him, he threw the box down, breaking five balls in the process. She paid for the whole box of balls, none of which she had wanted. I should never have let him bully me into bringing him, she thought.

Serves me right. Oh, God! She grabbed Mark's hand angrily and dragged him down the aisle.

"I don't wanna go!" he cried, and just as they got to the front door, he sat down, screaming.

"Get up this minute!"

"No!"

Shoppers turned to stare. Carol realized that she and Mark were providing one of those awful scenes that she'd always hated. She leaned down and picked Mark up, which was not an easy thing to do, for she had a heavy shopping bag and her purse, one on either arm, and he was a large, kicking three-and-a-half-year-old.

"You're hurting me, Mark. Stop it."

44

"I don't care," he yelled. But what he meant was, *Serves you right.*

It had begun to rain. She struggled down the street toward the parking lot. It must be three blocks away. The shopping bag had slipped to her wrist and was banging painfully against her knees. Her back ached from the weight of the struggling child. The rain was streaming down her forehead, mixing with angry tears.

"I gotta go to the potty!"

It was the final straw. She looked around for a filling station, but there was none in sight. The dime store was always snippy about letting little boys use the employees' washroom, and besides, she was already in trouble there. The department store was two blocks away in the wrong direction, so she chose the church. It was a large moldy-looking structure dedicated to Our Lady of Victory, which to the hopelessly overburdened mother, struggling with the heavy ground-floor door, seemed a fitting mockery.

There was no one about to ask directions of, so she pulled Mark along down the poorly lit corridor, looking for the rest room. The walls were covered with posters. Even in the half-light she began to walk faster to get past them.

"Wait, Mommy," Mark protested. She dropped the shopping bag and picked him up. The faces from the posters stared out at her. A black man looked out from behind bars. An old woman stared up from a nursing-home bed. A youth carrying a girl in his arms was fleeing from a bombed building. And the bloated belly of a Biafran child—the eyes staring at her as they had in the nightmare. . . .

She closed her own eyes until she got safely past the child, and when she opened them, she saw the rest room—comfort station, that's what her mother used to call it, a crazy old-fashioned name.

"I will not leave you comfortless." That was in the Bible somewhere. And it was a lie. She had been left comfortless. All those faces in the hallway . . . where was their comfort? They had been left comfortless, dying or rotting away.

She was putting Mark's snowsuit back on, but he was wriggling so that she couldn't fasten it.

"Stand still," she said harshly, not really to him but to that lie about comfort. I wish I could believe that God is dead, she thought. Because this way he is monstrous. "Stop wiggling, Mark," she said viciously.

Somewhere on the floor above the organist had begun to practice "Joy to the World! the Lord is come."

She picked up her purse and pulled open the bathroom door. Her shopping bag sat where she had left it at the far end of the haunted corridor. "This way, Mark," she said and started toward it, trying not to look at the posters.

She leaned down to pick up the bag, and as she straightened, she saw the caption under the black man's picture: "I was in prison and you came to me."

Mark had started in the wrong direction, poking the wall below the posters as he passed them down the hall.

"This way, Mark."

"No!" he said and began to run. She ran after him, past "I was sick . . . ," "I was naked . . . ," "I was hungry . . . ," up a dark staircase into a gloomy sanctuary. The organist was plodding through the refrain: "And wonders of his love, and won-ders, and won-on-on-ders o-of his love."

Mark was before the pulpit, reaching for a figure from the small wooden Nativity scene. "No!" she said, grabbing his chubby hand. "Don't touch it."

He looked up startled and then began to wail. Oh, God, it wasn't his fault. Poor little boy. God, God, why? Why is there nothing but misery? Mark could have posed for one of those posters.

I was in pain, and you did not comfort me.

She put her arms around him and looked up at the giant crucifix behind the altar. It was garishly realistic with red blood pouring from the wounded forehead, hands, side, and feet.

Serves you right, she thought. Serves you right, damn you! She would have screamed it aloud, if she'd been alone. She held Mark so close that his sobs were stifled in her coat. Where were you when I needed you? Where are you when anyone needs you? *Serves you right.*

The figure did not defend himself. He remained there, ugly and motionless, his head bowed deeply over his chest, his arms stretched out perpetually, his wounds forever fresh.

She began to weep for her dead child. Like the woman at the bottom of the cross. Like a million mothers in Vietnam and Ireland and Biafra.

Mark was tugging at her arm. "Look," he said. "Why don't they have a baby?"

She looked and saw that the manger in the Nativity scene held only straw. Carol dug a tissue from her purse and began to wipe Mark's face and then her own. She tried to explain that it wasn't Christmas yet; it was too early for the Baby to be put into the manger, but Mark was trying to puzzle it out on his own, his face wrinkled in concentration.

"Maybe God wanted Baby Jesus in heaven with him," he said at last.

"No," said Carol, looking once more into the bleeding face. "No, I don't think so."

She pulled Mark gently to his feet. *Serves you right.* The words had lost their nightmarish shriek. How had she ever thought she would be immune from suffering and death? She stroked her son's shining hair as she remembered again the faces in the downstairs corridor and felt within her a faint hope that she might learn somehow to serve them right.

Maggie's Gift

It all started because Mr. McGee didn't want to spend Christmas under a palm tree with a hula girl. Three weeks before Christmas, Barbara—his daughter—and her pleasant if frivolous husband, Jerald, had dropped their jobs and flown away to Hawaii. If the picture on the back of their postcard had been anything but a hula girl under a palm tree, he might have given their invitation to come join them in Hawaii a second thought. After all, he thought, as he spooned bean soup into a bowl and sat down for his meager lunch, after all, he'd spent the last three Christmases with them in the slush of Pittsburgh, in preference to his own lonely two-room apartment. But the hula girl was too much. When he looked at her, he felt an overwhelming need for ordinariness, for stability, for—heaven help him—a little dignity. Besides, he only had fifty dollars between him and his next social security check, and the idea of flying to Hawaii on Jerald's father's money was more than he could bear to contemplate.

In fact, he told himself for the fortieth time in less than three weeks, he would sooner have Christmas dinner alone at the Dairy Maid than celebrate courtesy of Jerald's doting father, who was not only several thousand times wealthier but ten years younger than Mr. McGee.

Still, as the days crept toward the twenty-fifth, he began to experience a little hollowness. His mind had turned more and more often to Christmases past, with little Barbara writing endless letters to Santa Claus and sweet-voiced May practicing her choir anthems at the old upright, rushing back to the kitchen to snatch ginger cookies out of the oven just in time. Ah, that was Christmas. The smell of ginger cookies and the music and the excitement of a little child. The huge tree that they had once cut themselves and then had to trim to get into the house. The gifts. For seven years straight, Barbara had given him a bottle of Aqua Velva and a pan of ginger cookies.

McGee, he said to himself. If you don't stop this nonsense, you'll be weeping into the bean soup. He leaned across the kitchen table and switched on the radio to give himself a little company.

". . . while for hundreds of area residents, this will not be a merry Christmas." The announcer's voice sounded to Mr. McGee like the pseudomournful tone of one who would soon be rushing home to his comfortable house in the suburbs. "They have no money for heating oil, much less toys for their children. . . ." To have children, to have a wife and family, and then not to be able to do for them—that must be terrible for a person. At least when May had been alive and Barbara home, he'd always been able to manage. How dare he feel sorry for himself? He had a little money. He could give Christmas to someone who wouldn't have it otherwise. Wasn't that what Christmas was all about? Who was that cute young woman who had spoken to the Retired Men's Fellowship at the church? Trainor. Miss Trainor. She was a sort of social worker for the area churches. She would be able to put him in touch with someone who needed his help. He was so eager he could hardly look up the number of the denominational office in the phone book. He dialed the number with a shaking finger.

"Yes?" said the voice on the other end.

"Merry Christmas." Mr. McGee tried to sound hearty.

"Yes?"

"Uh—" The voice was flustering him. "Miss—Miss Trainor?" he finally managed to stumble out.

"Will you hold, please?"

Miss Trainor was very polite. Yes, she remembered meeting Mr. McGee at the Fellowship meeting last week. How was he? Well, actually, the baskets-for-Christmas thing was really not the best idea. Sort of a handout. Demeaning to some people. Perhaps he'd like to make a donation to some ongoing work which would benefit the recipients more in the long run. He might, of course, try the Salvation Army or his own church.

Mr. McGee thanked her and hung up sadly. He didn't want to mail a check. He wanted to do something. It was just like those old sentimental poems that May had loved so much: He wanted to bring a real gift to the manger; he wanted to give himself.

He tried the church, but there the deacons had already made arrangements to take toys and dinners to nearby families. Would he like to make a contribution? Mr. McGee sighed and promised five of his fifty dollars.

His soup had gotten cold. He would have to reheat it if it was to be edible. Instead, he put a plate over the bowl and stuck it into the refrigerator.

He was about to commence a lecture on the pitfalls of self-pity when the phone rang.

"Yes?" he said.

"Merry Christmas, Mr. McGee!" It was cute little Miss Trainor again. "A problem has developed, and it just hit me that you might be the very person to help."

"Me?"

"Our church Children's Home in Reedsville tries very hard to make it possible for all the children there to go home for Christmas. In a few cases, of course, this is not possible, so we find a family that is willing to take the children in and share their Christmas with them. We have a brother and sister in the Reedsville Home. All the plans had been made for them to stay with a family here in the city, but the mother has just called. There has been a death in the family in Cleveland, so they will have to go to Ohio, which leaves our children without a place to go to. I would be glad to have them, but my fiancé and I are going to be with his parents in New York. . . ."

"So of course you can't take them." Mr. McGee was trying not to get excited.

"I know you're very active in your church, and I wondered if you knew anyone—"

"Know anyone? I—I can take them!" He was almost shouting.

"What about your wife, Mr. McGee? Are you sure she won't feel it's an intrusion?"

It was all Mr. McGee could do to keep from smiling heavenward. "I'm sure she'd be delighted," he said quite truthfully.

There was a pause at the other end of the wire. "I want you to know that ordinarily I make a careful check of every home that takes in our children, even for short periods."

"Oh, yes, yes, of course. But there's no time—"

"There's no time," she confirmed. "We'll need to have them picked up tomorrow morning. Please don't think me unprofessional."

"Never," he promised.

"The little girl is eight, and her brother is five."

"Perfect," he said.

"They, ah, they've been kicked around a bit, four or five foster homes before they landed at Reedsville, so, ah. . . ."

"Don't worry, Miss Trainor. I wasn't born"—he chuckled —"yesterday, you know. By the way, what color are they?"

"White." She sounded startled. "Does it matter?"

"Yes," he said. "I have to know what color to get the doll."

He sang his way through three department stores and a Woolworth's. The doll was a huge baby that opened and closed its eyes and cried "Mama." It cost four days of groceries. For the boy he got a shiny fire truck, which cost three days of groceries. There wasn't really money enough left for a turkey, but, he reasoned, there would only be the three of them, so he got a chicken. He'd be eating a lot of bean soup after Christmas, but he didn't care. The fire truck he chose was enormous. As he waited to pay for it, he clanged the bell until people stared.

"Merry Christmas!" he sang out to all the harassed clerks and grim-faced shoppers. He could hardly resist stopping total strangers to tell them of the Christmas gift he'd been given: Two children—two children who needed him.

The next morning Mr. McGee was up long before dawn. He took the bus to Miss Trainor's office and got there fifteen minutes early. He walked around the block, singing to himself, until it was time to go in.

The children were sitting side by side in straight chairs against the wall of her cubicle, their short legs dangling. Miss Trainor got up when he came in.

"Oh, Mr. McGee. It's so good to see you again." She shook his hand warmly. "This is Genevieve and this is Edgar Laughton." She indicated the children with her free hand.

Mr. McGee knelt down and put his arm across the back of Genevieve's chair. "Hi," he said gently. He didn't want to scare them. "I'm Mr. McGee, and I'm going to be your Christmas grandpa."

"The hell you say."

He stood up abruptly. "What did she say?" He couldn't believe his ears.

"I said," the little girl began, "the he—"

"Genevieve," Miss Trainor interrupted. "We've been all through this. Either you go with Mr. McGee, or you'll have to be the only children at the Home for Christmas."

"So?"

"You told me you wanted to go to the McGees'."

"I never!" Her eyes dared Miss Trainor to call her a liar.

"But, Genevieve," Mr. McGee pleaded. "You don't want to spend Christmas in an institution."

"I don't give a damn," she said mildly. "It's Edgar who don't like institutions."

They all turned to Edgar, who ducked his head and plugged up his mouth with his thumb and the corner of what had once been part of a blanket.

"Oh, all right, Edgar," Genevieve said, although Edgar had never opened his mouth except to put in his thumb. "If you're going to be so stubborn about it, we'll go with the dumb freak." She slid off the chair. Edgar did the same.

Miss Trainor coughed nervously. "Mr. McGee?"

"I'm sure everything will be fine, Miss Trainor," he said more confidently than he was feeling. "You just have a wonderful Christmas, hear?"

"Thank you, Mr. McGee," she said, handing him a small canvas bag, and she added quietly, "Good luck."

They emerged from the building into the sunlight. Genevieve glanced up and down. "Where's your car?"

"I—uh—don't have one anymore," he said.

"Ya hear that, Edgar? He don't even have a car."

"I thought you might enjoy riding the bus."

"Edgar wants you to know that our mother has six cars and two station wagons."

"Oh, is that right, Edgar?" Edgar continued sucking his thumb and playing with the frayed ends of his former blanket.

The apartment provided more material for Genevieve's contempt. "Two rooms? Where in the hell am I gonna sleep?"

"I thought you and Edgar could share the bed, and I'd take the couch."

"You gotta be outa your head. Edgar wets."

"Oh, well, we'll just have to rethink things."

"Edgar wants you to know that our mother has a house with sixteen rooms."

"And a château on the Riviera," mumbled Mr. McGee.

"Where's the TV? Edgar always watches TV."

Thank heavens for television, thought Mr. McGee. It might get them through. "It's in the bedroom," he said. "Shall I bring it in here for you?"

"You strong enough to carry a whole TV by yourself?"

"It's not very big," he said. And anticipating Edgar's next alleged complaint, he added, "It's black and white. I'm sure your mother's set is in full living color."

"Are you kidding? She got a color set in every room. Just ask Edgar if she don't."

"Edgar wants you to know that he ain't used to eating hot dogs," Genevieve informed Mr. McGee over the lunch table.

"Our mother always fixes us steaks and lemon meringue pie."

"I wish I'd known," said Mr. McGee. "My daughter used to love hot dogs."

"Edgar wants to know where your daughter's at."

"Hawaii," said Mr. McGee happily. Thank you, Barbara, for not being in Pittsburgh.

But Genevieve was undaunted. "Edgar wants you to know that our mother has eighteen children in eighteen different countries around the world. That's why she couldn't have us for Christmas. She was too busy visiting 'em all."

"I see," said Mr. McGee.

After lengthy consultations with Edgar, during which, of course, Edgar was never heard to speak, Genevieve determined that Edgar would deign to watch the eight-inch black and white set, since there was nothing better to do in this dumb joint.

Mr. McGee stretched out the dishwashing process as long as possible. What was he going to do? The thought of spending a quiet Christmas all by himself in these two rooms suddenly seemed cozy and extremely desirable.

The ladies on the game show were squealing with greed, and Genevieve shrieked directions. "Ya dumb mental! Take the box! Take the box! No! No! Ya weirdo! I tole ja! Take the box!"

Ah, the excitement of little children at Christmastime.

Genevieve got up at a commercial and came to the kitchenette. "Where's the loot?" she asked.

"The what?"

"You know, all the junk ya bought us."

57

He was seized with terror. What was going to happen when he gave Genevieve Laughton a baby doll in a pink voile dress that closed its eyes and cried "Mama"? He needed time. "Santa Claus won't be here until tomorrow." He decided not to add the line about good little boys and girls.

"Santa Claus? Aw, come off it, Maggie. Edgar ain't believed in Santa Claus since he was two years old."

"Well," he said, feeling for his own protection he'd better prepare her, "well, there isn't a great deal, but what there is, is for tomorrow morning."

"I don't get you, Maggie. Miss Trainor said you wanted us to come home with you so you could give us a happy Christmas. You ain't even got a Christmas tree. I betcha there ain't even any presents. Hell, at the Home, least they would give ya presents." She spun on her heel and went back to yelling at the TV-contest ladies.

Mr. McGee gulped down an Alka-Seltzer.

At about three the game shows turned into cartoons. "Get him! Get him! Beat him up!" Genevieve was screaming. Mr. McGee had not had such a headache since he'd gotten the telegram about Barbara and Jerald's elopement. Oh, Barbara, how is it under the peaceful palms with the lovely dancing ladies—the gentle pounding of the sea upon the sand?

"Get him! Kill him!"

Bravely, he assembled the ingredients for ginger cookies. The recipe written in May's curving hand nearly brought tears to his eyes.

Genevieve wandered over. "Whatcha think ya doing?"

"I am," he said, keeping his voice even with no little struggle, "making cookies. I thought you and Edgar might have fun helping me."

She raised an eyebrow. "Edgar wants you to know that he thinks it's sissy to make cookies."

Mr. McGee tried hard not to blame anyone when he eventually burned three out of the four pans of cookies.

"How come we're having bean soup for supper on Christmas Eve?" Genevieve sniffed and sneered when the bowls were served.

"I am sure your mother has filet mignon," Mr. McGee said. "But I am saving the *chicken,*" he emphasized the word, "for Christmas dinner, and this is the best I can do tonight."

"Edgar wants you to know ain't nobody can make him eat this slop."

Out of the corner of his eye, Mr. McGee noted with satisfaction that Edgar had put down his blanket long enough to pick up his spoon. "Nobody is going to make Edgar or *anyone else* eat anything." Mr. McGee fell to his soup and studiously ignored her.

"My mother," she said finally, "would die if she knew we was here."

So would mine, said Mr. McGee, but not out loud.

Genevieve flounced over to the couch and plopped down. "C'mon over here, Edgar," she said. "You don't have to eat that mess."

Edgar put down his spoon reluctantly.

"Leave Edgar alone," Mr. McGee said. "He's enjoying his supper."

"Listen here, Maggie, I don't know what you got in mind, but I ain't standing by letting my little brother poison hisself."

A foreign feeling was rising rapidly from Mr. McGee's gut. He belatedly recognized it as the urge to kill.

Edgar looked from one to the other, then poked his thumb and blanket back into his mouth and started for the couch. Genevieve smiled in triumph and patted the spot next to her. "Don't you be scared of nothing, Edgar. I'm going to take care of you." She snapped on the TV. Loud.

Mr. McGee took the room in three strides, turned off the set, and stood in front of the screen. "I can't stand any more TV tonight," he said.

"What in the devil ya expect us to do?"

"I do not expect you to do anything 'in the devil.' It is Christmas Eve." His voice was rising. "We are all going to church."

"Church! Ya gotta be kidding!"

"I have never been more serious in my life."

"Edgar wants you to know—"

"If Edgar wants me to know anything, he can tell me himself!"

"Boy—if my mother—"

"Your mother is not here. If I had the faintest notion where she might be found, believe me, I would call a cab and take you to her this very night. However, since she is unavailable, and Edgar is uncommunicative, it is just you and me, Gene-

vieve Laughton. I don't know about you, but I know about me
—I cannot take one more minute of your big-mouthed smarty
pants."

"Hey—Maggie—"

"Don't you dare 'hey, Maggie' me."

"Wait a—"

"Close your mouth. I am going into the bedroom and lie
down until time to go to church. If you dare turn this TV set
on, I will come in here and personally smack your bottom.
Understand?"

Edgar was nodding solemnly. Genevieve was staring at Mr.
McGee as though he had just plunked down from outer space.
Slowly she closed her wide-open mouth.

He slammed the door and flung himself across the bed. Oh,
Lord, forgive me. What was that verse about it being better
to have a millstone around your neck than a child? No. It was
better to have a millstone around your neck and be thrown
into the depths of the sea than to offend one of God's little
ones. Something like that. Genevieve, are you one of his little
ones? You?

The apartment was quiet except for the humming of the
refrigerator. The raging inside him began to calm a little. He
had almost drifted off, when he felt a presence above him. He
jerked awake. Edgar's smeared face hung just above his own.

"Genevieve," the little voice whispered. "He's alive."

Mr. McGee sat up and held out a hand toward the boy.
Edgar drew back shyly, but before he popped the thumb in,
Mr. McGee saw the mouth stretch into a tiny smile.

At church both Genevieve and Edgar were models of docility. Mr. McGee sang the carols with unusual gusto, pointing his finger to each word in the hymnal so Genevieve and Edgar could follow, but neither child tried to sing. They sat politely through the prayers and scriptures and sermon. Once Genevieve yanked Edgar's thumb out of his mouth, but she didn't speak.

After the service, he took them up front and showed them the crèche with its shepherds and wise men and tiny Baby Jesus, and the great tree with all its decorations, trying to make up a little for the barren apartment. They gazed solemnly at everything. Only once, when his friend little Mrs. Abernathy was gushing over his wonderfulness in taking these homeless children into his own home, did Mr. McGee catch Genevieve with a wry smile on her face. He smiled back.

The Abernathys drove them home afterward. Genevieve and Edgar sat on either side of him on the back seat, straight and silent. In the apartment he made some cocoa which the three of them sipped as they ate the few unburned ginger cookies.

"That's really weird, Maggie." Mr. McGee was so startled by the sound of Genevieve's voice after the hours of silence that he forgot to be offended by the nickname.

"What's weird, Genevieve?"

"Me and Edgar was born in City General."

"Yes?" Somehow that didn't seem too weird to Mr. McGee.

"Well, your Jesus guy didn't even have a place to get born in."

"That's right, Genevieve."

"It's like he was a foster kid before he was even born."

Mr. McGee swallowed. Out of the mouths of babes . . .

"Edgar! Whatcha got in your hand?"

Edgar tightened his fist, but Genevieve pried it open, finger by finger.

"Oh, Gawd," she said. "He's stole the Jesus from the church." She took the little plaster crèche figure and put it into Mr. McGee's hand, sighing deeply. Then she turned on the panic-stricken Edgar, who held his sucking thumb clenched between his teeth. "Maggie wants you to know, Edgar, that it ain't no use screaming for your mother. It's just you and me and him. And he is so mad at you he is about to personally smack your bottom." She turned to Mr. McGee with a proud smile for confirmation.

Mr. McGee didn't know whether to laugh or cry. Instead, he put his arm around the distraught little thief. "I don't think you meant to steal the baby, did you?"

Edgar looked up and shook his head solemnly.

"You see there, Genevieve, he didn't mean to steal the baby. He just didn't want Jesus to have to spend Christmas in an institution. Isn't that right, Edgar?"

Edgar nodded.

Genevieve shot Mr. McGee a quizzical look, but she didn't argue. And, as Mr. McGee wrote Barbara and Jerald the next day, the three of them had a great Christmas. Edgar loved the doll, and Genevieve never once claimed that their mother had fifteen much larger fire trucks stashed away in her country house.

Star of Night

It had been raining when he left Chicago, but now as the plane circled for landing, he could clearly see the picture-postcard dome bathed in light and the Washington Monument piercing white against the black winter sky. Against all his resolutions, the beauty of the city below made Carl hope that this trip would not be as futile as all the others.

The last time word of his son had come was two years ago. And then the message had been that Jimmy was dead. Even so, Carl had gone out to San Francisco, hoping at least to bring the boy's body home for burial, but there had been no trace of it. He had talked to two persons who had seen Jimmy taken to a hospital, unconscious from an overdose. They had not seen him again, but they had both heard that Jimmy had died.

When he first returned from the San Francisco trip, none of the family would believe that Jimmy was really dead. No death certificate was ever sent. But after a year with no word,

Carl noticed that the girls had begun to refer to Jimmy in the past tense, and lately both he and Miriam seemed to have come to an unspoken agreement to accept Jimmy's death as a fact.

And then suddenly yesterday, a phone call had come from one of Jimmy's high school friends. Jimmy was alive, he said. He had seen him on the street in Washington. Jimmy had pretended not to recognize him, but there was no doubt in the boy's mind that it was Jimmy he had seen.

Somehow—a miracle, the ticket agent said—Carl was able to get a reservation for Christmas Eve on a flight to Washington. He hated to leave Miriam and the girls, but their hope that he might bring Jimmy back home with him canceled their own disappointment. Carl himself resolved not to hope. His hopes had been shattered so often in the last five years that he carried the obliteration of hope about in his body like shrapnel fragments. He could not lay his weary soul open to still another assault of hope. And yet—and yet he did hope.

From the airport he called Bill Woodson, a fraternity brother, who was pastor of a large church in the city. After a brief tussle with the clergyman's protective secretary, he got through to his friend.

"Carl Porter!" the voice boomed, deeper and more resonant than Carl remembered it. "What brings you to Washington on Christmas Eve?"

"I heard yesterday that Jimmy might be here in the city."

"Jimmy? But I thought. . . ."

"Yes, so did we. But a school friend saw him here on the street a few days ago."

"But that's wonderful news!"

"Well, I hope so. I've got to find him first. I know how busy you must be, but I just don't know anyone else in the area who might help me."

There was a long pause at the other end of the line.

"I know this must be a bad time for you."

"Yes"—another pause—"I have another service tonight, and my wife has invited an army of relatives. . . . Have you tried the police?"

"No." Carl cleared his throat. "This is between me and Jimmy. I don't want to go to the police with it. . . ."

"Hey, why don't you come on over here? We'll put our heads together. I might think of someone who could help us with this thing."

"This thing" is my son, thought Carl, but he thanked Bill and got directions to the church.

Wearily he dumped his suitcase and umbrella into the front seat of the rented car. But as he drove, there unfolded before him a city more beautiful than the one he had seen from the air. Arlington stood in majesty above the Potomac, and Lincoln looked out in compassion over yet another generation of his confused children. The tree on the White House lawn was a gigantic tower of brilliant light, and the hope that he tried so hard to deny kept pushing up in his chest.

He left the car in a lot marked "For Staff Only" and took the back steps of the building two at a time. He was met by a custodian, and when he gave his name and asked to see the pastor, he was handed a note.

"Sorry. Had to rush home between services. Try Chris

Westoff at St. Thomas's. They work a lot with street people. Good luck and Merry Christmas!"

Street people. He swallowed and asked to be directed to a phone. He found the number for St. Thomas's and let it ring for what seemed an eternity. His only alternative was the police, and he dreaded having to go there. That was where the trouble between Jimmy and him had begun. No, not begun. It began God knew when. When had the boy changed from a laughing, bright little child into a stubborn, narrow-eyed enemy? He had tried to get through to the boy, God knows he had tried, but all their encounters ended alike—he, in a rage of frustration, driven to punish the child far more stringently than he had intended, while Jimmy looked at him coldly through those narrow slits and refused ever to cry.

That was why, as he had tried to explain to Miriam a hundred times, when Jimmy had called from the police station, Carl had waited until morning to go and get him. He had been unable to discipline the boy, perhaps a taste of the consequences would straighten Jimmy out. . . .

"St. Thomas's Church. Merry Christmas!" The background was such a din that he could hardly hear the speaker.

"Yes. This is Carl Porter. I'm trying to reach a Reverend Westoff."

"He's at a Christmas party right now. Can I take a message?"

"No. I'll come over. I have to see him." He checked the address in the phone book and on the way out got directions from the custodian. He had no difficulty suppressing his hope now as he opened the car door.

There was a form on the back seat. Carl felt more annoyed than startled. It would mean another delay in this endless search. "Who are you?"

"Man, don't you know better than to leave your car unlocked in this kind of neighborhood?" The form straightened up. Under the curly black hair, the face looked about twelve, maybe fourteen. It was hard to tell.

"What do you want?"

"Well, mainly, man, I want a warm place to sleep. My old lady went out and left the apartment locked up. If I break that lock again, she'll give me hell. I don't know when she'll be home. Tomorrow, next day, maybe. When she celebrates, man, she celebrates."

"What's your name, son?"

"Independence Murray. In honor of a little celebrating she did one Fourth of July."

"Oh."

"I don't mind. Suppose it had been Halloween?"

Carl got into the car and shut the door. "You know where St. Thomas's church is?"

"Nope."

"Want to help me find it?" It was a wild idea. The kid might mug him at the first dimly lit street.

"Hey, you're all right, man." Independence vaulted over into the front seat. He shoved the suitcase and umbrella toward the middle of the seat and settled himself comfortably in the corner.

Thus it was that when they finally found St. Thomas's, there were two of them. Carl was led through the din of a balloon race to a short man in a clerical collar. He was not sure how he could scream the tragedies of his life over the loud rock music and the shrieking voices and the bursting balloons. But the merciful pastor took the two of them to a closet-sized study and closed the door.

"I'm looking for my son. . . ." Carl saw at once that Westoff had heard the words a thousand times. He had not heard the name James or Jim or Jimmy Porter. The description Carl gave of the boy and the five-year-old picture must have sounded and looked like every other young boy the pastor had been asked about. It was to be another wild-goose chase. Rising, Carl tried to thank Westoff for his trouble.

"No, wait," the clergyman said. "We've just begun."

Westoff then spent about thirty minutes on the phone in a dozen undecipherable conversations. He seemed to spend a lot of time shaking his head. At last, in the midst of a conversation, he smiled and, putting his hand over the mouthpiece, turned to Carl.

"I have a lead on a boy that might be your son. Light brown hair, brown eyes, chipped front tooth. He's calling himself Brian Jones."

Carl's heart stopped as the huge poster of the Rolling Stones that Jimmy kept on his bedroom wall flashed before his eyes. "That sounds right. That could be Jimmy."

Westoff thanked the person at the other end of the line and hung up the receiver. "I think we're in luck," he said. "There's a girl here at the party that may be able to help us."

He reappeared shortly with a girl—a child, really—who wore a postage stamp of a dress. Her hair hung around her thin face and trailed almost to the abbreviated hem of her garment. She looked about twelve.

"I'm eighteen," she belligerently replied to Carl's stare.

"This is Tiny," Westoff said. "Tiny—Carl and Independence. Can you help them find Brian Jones?"

"I don't think Brian wants to be found too much."

"I just want to talk with him," Carl said.

She eyed him shrewdly.

"Come on, sister. Where's your Christmas spirit?" Independence asked.

The girl flashed Independence a sour look. "OK," she said to Carl. "I'll get my coat."

Tiny climbed into the back seat of the car, curled her legs under her, and settled into the corner with a cigarette.

"You'll have to direct me, Tiny." Carl started the engine.

"Yeah. Well, I don't know exactly where it is, but I think it's like toward Maryland. Northeast, you know."

Carl shifted carefully into reverse. He must keep his temper. This child was his only hope. He waited while she took a long puff from her cigarette.

"Try Thirteenth or Fourteenth Street," she said at last.

Independence knew enough to get them to Fourteenth Street and headed north. "Do you remember anything special about the place?" Carl concentrated on erasing any trace of impatience from his voice. "Any landmark that might help you recognize it?"

"Yeah. Like there's this big blinking star on a building

across the street from his house. If I hadn't been so stoned, it would have kept me awake all night."

Carl breathed audibly. "Good," he said. "We ought to be able to locate a sign like that."

They followed Fourteenth Street all the way into Maryland and Thirteenth all the way back. "Maybe they took it down," suggested the girl lackadaisically.

"Hey, wait a minute, man." Independence was leaning forward. "Stop at that drugstore over there."

Carl obeyed. The boy disappeared inside, and Carl had a fleeting fantasy of being the getaway man for Bonnie and Clyde. But in about ten minutes Independence reappeared, waving, not a sawed-off shotgun, but a piece of paper.

He forked it grandly over to Carl. "Here, man, is the name and address of the White Star Savings and Loan Corporation." He let Carl read the address and then slammed the door. "I had to go through a hell of a lot of stars in the yellow pages. But the way I figure it, with a big blinking star, it's got to be either a loan shark or an auto repair. Right?"

Carl started the car. "You're a genius, Independence."

The boy grinned happily. "So they tell me. So they tell me."

In less than five minutes they had found the White Star Savings and Loan. The cinder-block building seemed about to topple over under the weight of the huge star blinking on its roof.

Carl and Independence both turned to the back seat. "Well?" demanded the boy.

"Yeah," she said. "That's it. That house over there across the street—the one that's all boarded up."

"Don't look like nobody's living there."

"No, it don't," Tiny replied with light sarcasm and settled back into the corner for the return trip.

Carl got out. "You two can wait," he said. "I'm going to look around."

"In this neighborhood? You crazy, man?" Independence reached over and punched down the door lock, huddling down to make himself less conspicuous.

Carl walked around the house. He was feeling a little crazy. He had come so far across so many years and heartbreaks and gotten so close, only to lose again. It had once been an impressive house, in an ugly late-Victorian way, with two bay windows and massive front steps. All the windows on the first floor were boarded up, the panes long ago sacrificed to vandals. In the dim light he could see obscenities and slogans painted across the brownstone. There was a large official warning to trespassers posted on the front door. He rattled the doorknob, then banged on the door.

"Jimmy! Jim! Are you there?" It was no use. Fatigue assailed him as he turned to go back to the car.

Just then Independence jumped out of the front seat and ran toward him, grabbing his arm. "Look!" the boy whispered, pointing upward.

A thin wisp of smoke was rising from the chimney. They watched the old house in silence. Once Carl thought he saw something move at one of the second-floor windows. He turned to speak to Independence, but the boy was already back at the car. "OK, Tiny, out," Independence was saying.

He locked the door behind the reluctant girl. "You people

got ways of letting each other know who you are. How 'bout getting us into that house?"

"Yeah." Tiny shrugged Independence's hand off her arm. They followed her to the back of the house and up some steps to a small latticed back porch. "Got a credit card?"

Carl handed her one from his wallet, and she slipped it under the bolt through the crack of the screen door and yanked up. The door fell open. They followed her across the dark porch. She handed the card back to Carl and then knocked on the door in what he guessed was a code. There was a scuffling noise inside, then silence. At length the door opened a crack.

"Oh, Tiny, it's you, isn't it?" a soft voice replied. The crack was widening to reveal a girl even more pale and childlike than Tiny. Her dark hair hung almost to her waist. She wore a long beaded dress. In her left hand she was carrying a candle, which gave her features a soft warmth, and slung over her right hip was a baby wrapped in a fringed shawl.

"Who is he?" She pointed her candle past Tiny.

"It's all right," said Carl. "He's with me."

Independence jabbed him in the ribs. "She means you, baby. Not me." Carl blushed in the darkness. Of course, the boy was right. It was Carl himself who was suspect in this setting.

"It's all right, sister," Independence said jauntily. "We're just the three wise guys following the big blinking star. How about a little shelter for dusty travelers?"

The solemn little mother smiled. "I thought they were three men—wise men."

73

"So? We're liberated. Right, Tiny?" By this time Independence had smooth-talked his way through the door and was standing beside the girl. With a bow he shoved the door wide and ushered Tiny and Carl into the house. The girl made no objections. They followed her and the candle through the ancient kitchen and broad hallway into what must have been the parlor. Through the cracks in the boards, the star of the loan company across the street gave a steady pulse of light. There was a large fireplace in the room, built for four- or five-foot logs. In it, a tiny orphaned flame sputtered. The only furniture was a mattress pushed against the wall. The girl put the candle on the floor and shifted the baby to her other hip.

"Seen Brian lately?" Tiny asked finally. She pointed her nose at Carl. "Says he's his old man. Just wants to talk."

"Really, I do just want to talk with him," said Carl. He tried to keep from begging, but the tone came through all the same.

"Let's just sit down," suggested Independence, plopping himself down on the mattress.

Carl sat on the floor near the girl. She was toying with the fringe on the baby's shawl.

The baby was quiet, but the girl hugged it to her as though it needed comforting. She looked into the little face and said quietly, "Brian, Brian is dead."

He had heard it before, and he hadn't believed it then, either. So although the word "dead" bound his chest like a cold chain, Carl did not surrender to it.

"When did he die?"

"October," the girl replied. "November." She was talking

to the baby rather than to him. "We don't always know the time, do we, Jason?"

"Was it drugs?"

The girl looked up quickly. "No," she said. "He's been clean since Frisco. He nearly died in Frisco."

"I heard that."

"No. He was looking for work. He was worried about me and the baby, you know. A car hit him. . . ."

The floor creaked above their heads. Carl looked up. "Rats," said the girl. The baby made a gurgling noise.

"Hey, can I hold him?" asked Independence.

"He might cry," said the girl.

"No way. Babies are crazy about me." Independence leaned over and took the child. "Hey, he's really something. How you doing, man?" The baby smiled up at the boy and made more baby noises. "See that? He's laughing." The boy began to sing under his breath, rocking himself and the baby in rhythm:

> *"Mary had a baby, yes, my Lord,*
> *Mary had a baby, yes, my Lord,*
> *Mary had a baby, yes, my Lord,*
> *The people keep a-coming and the train has gone."*

"I always liked that part about the train," Independence explained to no one in particular and resumed his quiet song.

Carl leaned toward the girl. "May I ask you another question?"

"Sure," said the girl, not taking her eyes off the boy and the baby.

"Is the baby—is Jason my . . . ?"

"He's Brian's, yes." She turned toward him with a half smile. "I don't mind if you don't."

"No, no," he stammered. "I'm—I'm very pleased—proud. . . ."

"You hear that, Jason baby?" the boy asked. "You just got yourself a proud granddaddy. Want to hold him?"

"Well, I—"

"Hey, don't be scared, Carl baby. Jason won't hurt you." He handed the baby to him.

Carl trembled at the touch. He looked into the baby's face, searching there for something of Jimmy. The baby smiled. I'm going to cry, thought Carl. When have I ever cried?

"Hey"—Tiny was on her feet—"hey, can we go now? I got you here like I said."

Carl opened his mouth to reply but shut it again as a huge rat emerged from the darkness and raced across the floor toward them. They all drew back as it ran over the mattress and into a hole in the wall on the other side.

"Wow," said Independence respectfully. "They grow 'em big around here, don't they?"

"Yes," said the girl. Carl could see that she was shivering.

"Come with us," he said. "Let me find you a warm place to stay—without any rats."

"We don't stay here all the time, you know"—Her jaw was out—"just until we can get enough for key money on a decent place."

"I know," said Carl. "But let me help you just for a few days, anyway."

"No, I can't leave."

"Are you waiting for Jim—for Brian, I mean?"

"Didn't I already tell you Brian is dead?" She wouldn't look at him.

"You're waiting for someone else?" he asked gently.

"No."

"Please, come with us—for Jason's sake."

"I can't leave." She reached out, so Carl reluctantly gave her the baby. She hugged him close.

Carl turned to the boy. "Independence, would you get my things from the car?"—he handed him the keys—"We'll spend the rest of the night here."

"What a hell of a way to spend Christmas," grumbled Tiny.

Independence flipped the keys into the air with his left hand and caught them behind his back with his right. "You can always hoof it on your own, Tiny baby."

"In this neighborhood? You crazy, man?"

Carl distributed the clothes from his suitcase. The girls and baby lay down on the mattress covered with a ragged blanket, Carl's overcoat, and his extra suit jacket and pants. Independence lay near the fireplace on top of part of the *Chicago Tribune* and put another section over him.

At everyone's insistence, Carl himself put on his bathrobe over his suit and then propped himself in a corner with the umbrella next to him. He was determined not to sleep and was sure, in fact, that the cold would keep him awake, but despite his discomfort exhaustion overcame him. Toward dawn his

77

head had dropped to his chest, and he was dozing, when he heard the clicking noise of rat paws on the wooden floor. By the time he was fully awake, the rat was nosing about the mattress near the baby's face.

Carl jumped to his feet with a shout, expecting the rat to run, but the creature snarled like a vicious little dog and turned its attention once more to the child.

It was not just a hungry animal to Carl. It was some evil manifestation. It was all the evil in himself, and in everyone like him, that brought these little children to such a place. And Carl attacked it as such.

He swung the heavy handle of the umbrella down with such force that the rat gave out an almost human shriek and then lay stunned. Carl kicked it away from the mattress. He tried to stab it with the point of the umbrella, but the flesh was soft and gave way under his blows, so he raised his foot and stamped down again and again with his heel until dark blood gushed from the rat's head and ran onto the floor. The creature twitched, then was still. With the point of his umbrella Carl pushed the rat's body into the fireplace.

Panting, the sweat rolling from under his bathrobe, Carl fell back into his corner.

"Jesus"—Independence was staring at him respectfully—"you're in the wrong line of work, man."

They were all staring at him. Carl wiped his sweating hands on his bathrobe. He was ashamed for them to look at him like this.

There was a noise on the stair. Oh, God, he wasn't up to another battle, but he staggered to his feet and raised his umbrella against this new intruder. This one was human, with shoulder-length brown hair and a beard.

"Take it easy, Dad." The speaker had a chipped front tooth.

"Jimmy?" Carl lowered the umbrella.

The young man went over to the mattress and bent over the girl, who was now holding the screaming child. "Is he OK?" he asked.

"Yes," she said.

"It's all right, Jason boy," Jimmy said soothingly, stroking the tiny cheek with his forefinger. "It's all right."

"I think he's just hungry," said the girl. She unhooked her dress and began to nurse the baby.

"We thought you were dead, Jimmy," Carl said.

"I was, in a way. I'm all right now."

"Why couldn't you let us know? Would it have been so hard just to call your mother?"

"Not hard to call Mother. No."

"Oh, God." Carl turned away. He was sobbing.

Strong young arms came about his shoulders. "Sh-sh. It's all right. You came to look for me, didn't you?" Jimmy held Carl tightly. "I saw you fighting for my baby," he said softly. "I was watching through the floor."

"Well," said Independence. "This is a nice little scene, but I gotta move on to the next act. Come on, Tiny. Hand me those things." He started to pack Carl's suitcase.

"Come back home with me, Jimmy."

The young man shook his head. "Not now," he said. "In the spring we'll come."

"Would you let me lend you the deposit for an apartment?"

Jimmy looked quickly at the rat where it lay in the cold fireplace. "That would be good, Dad. I'd appreciate it. Just until spring." He smiled his boyish chipped-tooth smile.

"I'd appreciate a little breakfast," Tiny's shrill voice announced.

"He's taking us all out to breakfast, Tiny. Don't you worry. Little celebration due all round." Independence immediately took charge of herding the little group out the door and toward the car.

Across the street, the White Star Savings and Loan Corporation squatted small and dirty under its darkened star.

"Right on, guiding star!" Independence waved. "We wise guys have seen the light."

"Yeah," said Tiny. "Ho, ho, ho! Merry Christmas and all that."

Carl put his arm around the girl's thin shoulders. "Merry Christmas to you, too, Tiny," he said.

He Came Down

Lydia sat alone in the back row of the drafty old sanctuary and tried to concentrate on the rehearsal. A skinny brown boy in a plaid bathrobe had raised a broomstick masquerading as a shepherd's crook, and was shouting at the top of his lungs, "There's a star in the East on Christmas morn!"

"Rise up, shepherds, and follow!" his straggly band of bathrobed companions chorused.

"No, no, no!" Stephen's voice came out of the dark somewhere. "Don't yell it, Sammy. Sing it. Now, let's see a little joy on your faces, boys. This is good news. Jesus is born. OK. Try it again."

Good news. How long had it been since any news had been good? Lydia pulled her coat with its great fur collar closer about her. She knew it had been a mistake to come to spend Christmas with Stephen, but he did not want her to stay in

Cambridge alone in that enormous house where for the past year she had watched her husband die.

So she had come, as her son had ordered her to, but she had not been able to explain to him how the year had been or how she who had always been so complete and sure had become a hollow frame.

In the beginning she had prayed. Oh, how she had prayed! But then her prayers had turned to angry questionings until, when Frank died, her faith had died with her fury. And even now, watching Stephen talking earnestly with his would-be shepherds, she felt nothing—neither the old pride that he had become a minister, nor the more recent resentment that his youth and brilliance were being wasted in this Godforsaken place.

The building was the castoff of a once wealthy congregation. It was a gloomy nineteenth-century Gothic building that defied adequate lighting and heat. There were bits of pasteboard here and there, covering the spots where vandals had broken panes in the stained-glass windows, so that the Good Shepherd looked down tenderly on a lamb that lacked a head. And there was no baby in the manger—only the side of a paper carton to keep out the cold.

"How're you doing?" Stephen slid into the pew beside her. He smiled, then turned his eyes back to the rehearsal as he spoke. "Could I ask an enormous favor of you?"

He hadn't asked her for anything in years. "What is it?"

"Our Mary hasn't shown up for rehearsal, and it may mean she won't get here for the performance either, unless. . . . Her father was killed in November, and her poor mother has been in and out of the hospital. Dolores is probably baby-sitting for her baby brother again. I know it's a lot to ask. Everything here is so different from what you're used to. . . ."

She could feel herself bristling. "I imagine I could sit with a baby for an hour or two without falling to pieces, if that's what you mean."

He patted her hand. "I'm not worried about your credentials as a sitter," he said. "It's a rough neighborhood. If there was anyone else I could ask at the last minute. . . ."

She stood up. "How do I get there?"

"I'll ask Russell to walk you over." He indicated a tall black boy waiting in the aisle. "Double-lock the door, all right?"

Lydia nodded.

"I hate for you to miss the program."

"I don't mind," she said truthfully and followed Russell out into the cold winter afternoon.

It was dark already, and she walked faster to keep pace with the long-legged boy. He slowed down but did not speak.

"Is it far?" she asked.

He shook his head. In the narrow street, horns squawked and drivers cursed as they tried to maneuver past one another between the two lines of parked cars. A group of children had turned the sidewalk into an enormous hopscotch game. It was too dark to see the lines, but they kept on playing, screaming in argument over violations, real or imagined. A man came weaving down the sidewalk toward them. Russell touched her arm lightly to steer her safely past him.

"It's here, Miz Paxton." She followed him up the stone steps and into the front hall. The row house had once been fashionable, but now when Russell opened the door, they were engulfed by an odor. So this is what poverty smells like, she thought.

"It's upstairs." She followed him up two flights, trying to concentrate on the back of his raincoat and not on the smell. As they went down the dark hall, she saw at the end the communal toilet with a bare light bulb hanging from the ceiling.

"Dolores," Russell called as he knocked. "S'me, Russell. Preacher sent me to get you for the show."

The door opened a crack. The large eyes in the tan face looked past Russell and at Lydia. Old eyes in a thin, young face.

"This Miz Paxton, Preacher's mother. Preacher says she can stay here with the baby."

Still the girl hesitated. A woman's querulous voice called to her in Spanish. The girl turned her head toward the voice and replied in Spanish.

Russell interrupted. "Let me tell her, Dolores. You supposed to be there a hour ago."

Dolores let them into the dimly lit room. On the one bed lay her mother, her thin face screwed up in pain and annoyance. Above her head was the room's only touch of color—a garish plaster crucifix.

"She gotta come to church, Miz Mendez," Russell said. "She's Mary."

The woman struggled for his meaning and then turned to the girl, who interpreted the boy's words. Something within the woman's face relaxed a little. She murmured to the girl.

"Miz Paxton will watch your boy, Miz Mendez. You don't have to worry 'bout nothing."

Dolores interpreted once more, then turned back smiling. "She wants me to be the Virgin. She's very proud." She looked at Lydia shyly. "I hope the baby won't be trouble."

"No, no, I'm sure," Lydia mumbled.

The boy and girl left quickly then. She could hear their laughter as they ran down the hall and bounced down the rickety stairs. The heavy front door clanged shut behind them.

Well, thought Lydia as she double-locked the door, now what? She had somehow imagined that the mother would be in the hospital. Not here, at any rate. Lydia could feel the great dark eyes following her about the room. She tried to smile at them, but there was no response. Should she take off her coat? The room felt colder than the street outside. Still, it might appear rude to keep it on. She had seen how Mrs. Mendez looked at the coat, her eyes narrow and calculating as they rested on the fur collar, but in the end she left it on. It was the last gift Frank had given her, and it promised both warmth and protection in this bitter place.

"The baby?"

Mrs. Mendez understood and drew a bundled form from under her quilt. She should not have asked. The child, who had been sleeping peacefully against the warmth of his mother's body, began to howl with anger at being so suddenly and coldly awakened. The more he howled, the more agitated his mother became, until at last she was screaming at him in

Spanish. And then, to Lydia's consternation, she turned to her, screaming in fury.

Lydia stepped back toward the door. Was the woman ordering her out? But Stephen must have sent her here because he feared the woman would be in no condition to care for the baby. So Lydia simply stood there, letting the stream of anger pour over her, until, at last, it was spent and the exhausted woman turned her face to the wall, leaving the still-crying baby on the edge of the bed.

In a moment of paralyzed horror, Lydia watched the tiny struggling form rock and rock and then throw itself over. She jumped just as he fell toward the floor and caught him by the arm. The terrified child howled all the louder. Mrs. Mendez never moved her head.

Lydia's own fear now turned to rage at the unmoving figure. "You stupid woman!" she cried at the hump in the quilt. "He nearly fell off the bed. He could have broken his neck."

Mrs. Mendez made no reply. But the burst of anger seemed to release Lydia for action. She tucked the screaming baby under her arm, football fashion, and began to poke around the room for a change of clothes. She could find nothing that seemed to be diapers or indeed any baby things. At last she found half a torn sheet. It would have to do. It was too cold to leave him wet. She put him on the metal table and wrestled off the wet clothes. Then she wound the sheet about him from his neck to his toes, arms and all. The child, suddenly dry and warm and unable to kick or thrash, stopped his screams for a moment and stared up at her.

The quiet was short-lived. Soon the child started to scream

again. Lydia began to whistle under her breath as she carried him into the corner of the room that served as kitchen. Dolores had not failed her here. In the ancient refrigerator was a bottle of milk. She pulled a chair close to the stove while she heated the milk.

The cries stopped the moment she popped the bottle into the small mouth. With a feeling of triumph Lydia watched the baby greedily sucking the nipple. The little head on her arm was covered with black silky hair. Stephen had been so fair as a baby. She leaned over and rubbed the hair with her cheek.

The boy let the empty bottle fall from his mouth and snuggled nearer to her. Lydia held him close and began to hum under her breath.

She did not choose the tune consciously. It was "Once in Royal David's City," the hymn that had always been Stephen's lullaby. Suddenly, as she hummed, the words came to her clearly.

> *He came down to earth from heaven,*
> *Who is God and Lord of all,*
> *And his shelter was a stable,*
> *And his cradle was a stall;*
> *With the poor, and mean, and lowly,*
> *Lived on earth our Saviour holy.*

"With the poor, and mean, and lowly." And then she saw the scene as it must have been. Not the gentle beasts kneeling in the sweet-smelling hay about the haloed family, but a real woman far away from home, bringing a child to birth in a damp, cold cave filled with the smell of the animals who were stabled there.

She felt Mrs. Mendez's stare before she actually turned to see the woman sitting up in bed. Her eyes were afire with hatred. When Lydia turned to her, she began a quiet chant in bitter Spanish. Gradually the tempo and volume increased. The power of her anger grew until her frail body shook. Then a thin arm shot up and snatched the plaster crucifix from the wall.

Warily Lydia stood up, holding the child close. She moved sideways across the end of the room until she had put the table between herself and the strange, tortured creature on the bed.

The arm went back. Lydia, shielding the baby in her arms, ducked and the crucifix crashed on the wall above her head. The baby screamed out.

"Sh-sh," Lydia said to the child. As she straightened, the fragments of plaster on her back dropped lightly to the linoleum. At her feet lay the head crowned with bloody thorns. With a shiver she turned to face Mrs. Mendez and found herself staring into a dark mirror. There in the eyes across the room was the same rage, the fear, the awful emptiness she knew so well.

The baby was crying harder. Lydia stepped across the shattered remains of the crucifix, around the table, to the bed where the other woman sat, her breathing harsh and irregular from the exertion of hurling the plaster figure.

"Here, Mrs. Mendez." Lydia sat down on the edge of the bed and handed the child to her. "He needs you."

Dumbly the woman took her son. She began to rock him gently and to hum. Gradually, as she rocked, her eyes lost their desolation and became warm and human. When at last the child was sleeping on her breast, she looked once more at Lydia. "So nice," she said, reaching over shyly to stroke the fur collar of Lydia's coat.

"Like your baby's hair," said Lydia, and both of them touched the little head.

Stephen brought Dolores home, and they brought with them the joy of the pageant, the flush of success (for it had gone better than any rehearsal had let them dream it might), little jokes of near mishaps, and unexpected reactions from the audience (many of whom had simply come in from the cold and were startled to find themselves in Bethlehem). Dolores translated for her mother, hesitantly at first, but then happily as her mother nodded and smiled encouragement.

Suddenly the girl stopped. She had spied the plaster fragments Lydia had swept up earlier and discarded in the waste can. Dolores looked in alarm first at her mother and then at Lydia. "What happened?" she asked. "The crucifix . . ."

"He came down," Lydia said aloud, and then to herself, *He came down—even to me.*

Woodrow Kennington Works Practically a Miracle

"The first thing I see when I open the door is Sara Jane lying on the rug with my stamp collection all over the place." Woodrow was sitting on the curb in front of his house trying to explain the tragic events of the past hour to his friend Ralph. "My *stamp* collection!"

Ralph was doing his best to sound sympathetic. "Geez," he said.

"I start screaming like an idiot, 'What the hell you think you're doing?' She says—you know how she sticks up her eyebrow—only five-year-old I ever heard of could poke up one eyebrow—she says, cool as can be, 'Hi, Whoodrow.' Blowing my name out like birthday candles. 'Hi, Whoodrow. I'm playing post office.' *Post office!*" Woodrow bent over in pain. "Post office with practically priceless stamps I inherited from my grandfather. I was practically crying out loud. 'Why? Why?'" Woodrow spread out both arms, imitating himself. " 'Why are you playing post office with my stamps?' "

"And she says?"

"She says—get this—she says, 'Don't be stoopid, Whoodrow. You gotta have stamps to play post office.' "

"Oh, yeah?" Ralph grinned and poked him in the ribs with an elbow. "Just ask Jennifer Leonard."

"Shut up, Ralph. You haven't even heard the worst part yet."

Ralph tried to get properly serious. "There's a worst part?"

"About this time my mother comes rushing in, in a bathrobe. It is three thirty in the afternoon. My sister has destroyed an entire fortune in rare stamps while my mother has been taking a nap."

"Yeah?"

"The *reason* she has been taking a nap and let my juvenile-delinquent sister run wild—she takes me off to the den and shuts the door to tell me this goody—the reason she laid down and took her eye off Sara Jane 'for one minute' is that she is pregnant."

"Yeah?"

"My mother is thirty-eight years old."

"So?"

"Ralph, she is too old already to handle Sara Jane."

At about eight that evening Ralph called. After the usual questions about homework had been taken care of, he said, "You know I been thinking about what you told me. I don't think you should be too upset."

"Ralph! That was a practically priceless stamp collection!"

"No, I don't mean about the stamps. I mean about becoming a brother again. Wood, face it. You got no place to go but up, man. When this next kid is five, you're sixteen. Sixteen. You know what a sixteen-year-old guy looks like to a five-year-old? Geez. This kid is liable to worship you."

It was not the worst idea Ralph had ever had. In fact, the more Woodrow thought about it, the better it sounded. His mother was surprised and delighted when he started going out of his way to help her. She began to treat him more and more like an adult. She even asked him to try to get Sara Jane to accept the idea of a new baby.

This was no small problem. Sara Jane had expressed neither excitement nor resentment when they told her. She simply pretended that she hadn't heard. Once when he was baby-sitting, Woodrow tried very hard to explain the whole situation to her. He even threw in a few interesting facts of life as a bonus.

"Don't be stoopid, Whoodrow." She never mentioned the subject again, or even seemed to hear others mention it, until the day she found Woodrow and his mother putting together the old baby bed in her room.

She marched in, hands on hips. "Get this junk outta my room."

"Sara Jane, it's for the baby." Mother was super patient. "You remember, I talked to you yesterday . . ."

"I'm not having no baby."

"We're all having a baby, Sara Jane."

"Not me."

"OK. *I'm* having a baby, but . . ."

"Then put this junk in your own room."

"But darling, I explained, there's no place. . . ."

Woodrow offered on the spot to take the baby into his room. His mother stalled and his father fumed, but eventually the bed, bureau, and rocking chair took the place of his racing-car setup. His father bought a screen and covered it with airline posters, but he needn't have. Woodrow was not feeling anything like a martyr. It was the chance of a lifetime. He would start this kid out right. No more Sara Janes for him.

As for Sara Jane, she would come to Woodrow's door and stand there with her hands on her hips, her eyebrow elevated, staring at the crib legs peeking out below the bottom of the screen, but she never said a word. Occasionally, though, she would sigh—a sigh as long and weary as the *whooo-oosh* of his mother's ancient percolator. It made Woodrow uneasy, but not prepared for what happened next. He wondered later if he should have been prepared. Shouldn't he have taken a cue from her strange shift in TV programs? What normal kid would move in the span of two weeks from *Electric Company* to *Speed Racer* to, of all things, *The One True Word,* starring Brother Austin Barnes? He had really meant to ask her about it, but the switch took place in the last wild days before the baby was born, and frankly, everyone was so glad to have her quiet and occupied that they neglected to keep a proper check on what she was watching.

When his father called from the hospital at seven o'clock to tell him that he had a brother, Woodrow let out a whoop that could have been heard for blocks. It brought Sara Jane out of the den into the kitchen. "It's a boy!" Woodrow yelled at her. "A boy!"

She watched him with a very peculiar expression on her face —neither anger nor surprise, certainly not delight. Where had he seen it before? A memory of old fading pictures in the back of the Sunday School closet came to his mind—it was that same sickly sweet half smile.

Then she let him have it. "Brother Whoodrow," she said. "I saw Jesus today."

"You what?"

Her smile, if anything, got more sickly. "I said, 'I saw Jesus.'"

Surely it was that religious program she had been watching —that combined with the shock of the news he had just given her. He felt very generous, almost sorry for her, so he tried to be kindly. "So you saw Jesus, huh?"

"I was walking home from school. All alone. Nobody meets me halfway anymore. Mommy got too fat, and Mrs. Judson is too lazy." She paused to let these sad words sink in. "But Jesus loves me. Just like Brother Austin says. When Jesus saw me coming home from school, he stopped his big black car. 'Hi,' he says."

"Sara Jane, that wasn't Jesus. He never had any big black car."

"He does now."

Woodrow was beginning to feel panicky. "Did he ask you to get into the car or anything?"

"No," she said primly.

He was not about to let Sara Jane get kidnapped while his

mother was in the hospital. He told Mrs. Judson, who was staying there days, that Sara Jane had to be met at the school door. Mrs. Judson read one of those newspapers that never hesitate to give all the gory details, so when he told her about the big black car, she made the trip to the kindergarten door every day, lazy or not.

In the meantime, Daniel came home. He was the greatest baby in the world, even when he cried. In fact, Woodrow's favorite time was when Daniel cried at two o'clock in the morning. His mother would fuss and apologize when she'd come in and find Woodrow awake, but then they'd talk while she fed the baby. What a warm, good feeling to be talking in the middle of the night—grown-up to grown-up. It would have been the happiest time of his life except for Sara Jane.

He may have saved her from kidnapping, but he certainly hadn't solved the real problem. He wasn't sure if he was going to be able to stand it. Sara Jane the screaming baby, he had endured. Sara Jane the unbearable brat, he had gotten more or less used to. But Sara Jane the Saint was about to do him in.

Ralph thought it was the funniest thing since Whoopee cushions, but he didn't have to live with her. She was always smiling at him and calling him Brother Whoodrow and begging him to watch *The One True Word* with her. She prayed all the time. If Mrs. Judson fussed at her, she would go into her room and fall on her knees, praying that God would forgive poor bad Mrs. Judson. It was Woodrow's job to fix breakfast for the two of them. Sara Jane would bless the food until the toast had turned to floor tile.

But even that he might have put up with had she not announced to him one morning that their parents were going to Hell.

"Shut up, Sara Jane."

"But they're lost!" she said.

"They are not lost. They're Presbyterians."

"See? They don't even know they're lost and going to Hell."

"Well, why don't you just tell them?"

"They'd laugh at me."

They would, too. He wanted to laugh himself, but he couldn't quite. Suppose his father and mother were headed for Hell and didn't even know it? Suppose he were? They were all bound for Hell while Sara Jane. . . . Suddenly, as the robots would say, it did not compute. Sara Jane the Saint was pure plastic—the fake of all fakes. Instead of letting her scare him, he should be whipping her back into shape. It was up to him to get her back to normal. Normal, mind you, was never all that great, but normal he could manage.

First, he would silence *The One True Word*. Fortunately, the TV set was practically an antique, which meant all he had to do was take a couple of tubes out of the back and hide them in his bureau drawer beneath his underwear.

When Sara Jane complained to her father that the TV was broken, he hardly looked up from his newspaper. He didn't like TV anyhow, which was why he'd never bothered to get a decent set, much less color.

"Who is going to fix the TV?" she persisted.

Her father put down his paper. "Nobody has time to bother with that TV before Christmas. Besides"—he was already back behind the paper—"you watch too much TV anyway."

Woodrow found her some minutes later on her knees in the den, her hand on the cold set. "O Lord"—Woodrow wasn't sure if she were praying aloud for his benefit or God's—"O Lord, make this TV set well. The Devil broke it, but you can make it well."

"Sara Jane!" He was so shocked that he burst right into her prayer. She ignored him and kept on rocking and praying. Woodrow was not crazy about being called the Devil, but he sure as heck was not going to put the tubes back now and turn the kid into a permanent religious weirdo.

Next morning at breakfast, there were no lengthy announcements. Sara Jane just rolled her eyes up at the ceiling and said, "OK, God. You know what you gotta do." And in answer to Woodrow's openmouthed stare, she said, "He knows if he doesn't hurry up and fix that set, I'm not going to believe in him anymore."

When he came in from school two days in a row to find her praying over the TV set, he began to weaken. "How about me taking you Christmas shopping, Sara Jane?"

Slowly she turned and gave him her saddest face. "I guess I'm not going to believe in Christmas this year. The TV still doesn't work."

"Oh"—his voice sounded very cheery and very fakey—"I wouldn't give up on Christmas just because of some old TV. Maybe it's just a broken tube or something."

"God can do anything he wants to. If he doesn't want to fix this TV, it means he doesn't want me to be his child. I guess nobody wants me to be their child."

Ralph, after he stopped laughing, suggested that Woodrow launch a campaign. It was obvious that the child felt insecure. Woodrow needed to prove to her that her family really loved her. Then she would be cured.

Woodrow was desperate enough to try anything, even a suggestion from Ralph. He persuaded his mother that she was not too tired to make cookies with Sara Jane, since he, Woodrow, would clean up the entire kitchen afterward. Sara Jane made twelve gorgeous gingerbread men, all scowling. Woodrow talked his father into taking Sara Jane on a special trip to see Santa Claus. She had climbed, after much urging, onto the old fellow's lap, only to ask him why his breath smelled all mediciny. Woodrow himself devoted a full Saturday morning to helping Sara Jane make a crèche out of baker's dough.

"Sara Jane." He tried not to sound too critical. "We can't use fourteen snakes in one manger scene."

"That's all I feel like making, Whoodrow. Just snakes and snakes"—she sighed—"Dead snakes."

"Suppose," he said, his eyes carefully on the sheep he was modeling, "suppose the TV would get well. Would you feel better then?"

"It's too late. God flunked already."

"Maybe he just needed a little more time, or something."

She looked him dead in the eye. "If the TV got fixed now,

I'd know it was you or daddy did it. Just to shut me up. You're just scared I'm going to mess up your old Christmas. That's all you care about."

He tried to protest, but she was too close to the truth. How could he enjoy Christmas when he felt like some kind of a monster?

Christmas Eve their parents went off to church, leaving him in charge. There had been a bit of trouble earlier when Sara Jane had refused at first to hang up her stocking. "I just don't believe in Christmas anymore," she had said wearily. Their parents hadn't known whether to take her seriously or not, but Woodrow had. He whispered in her ear that if she didn't hang up her stocking that minute he was going to beat the you-know-what out of her the minute the folks walked out the door. She sighed, that long now-frequent sigh of hers, and handed him her stocking to put up.

After he had gotten her, still moaning and sighing, into bed, he sank into the big living-room chair, staring miserably at the blinking lights of the Christmas tree. The tree itself looked so fat and jolly and merry that he was close to tears when the telephone rang.

It was Ralph. He was baby-sitting, too, but he was so cheerful it made Woodrow feel murderous. "Say, there's this great movie on Channel Seven. It was practically X-rated when it first came out."

"Our TV's broken, remember?"

Ralph chortled. "I also remember, old buddy, that you can work that little miracle whenever you want to."

Woodrow slammed down the receiver. Everything always

seemed simple to Ralph. When Ralph looked at his Christmas tree, he didn't have to see at its base fourteen dead snakes guarding a manger scene. If only he could fix everything as easily as he could fix that blasted TV. Well, what the heck? A practically X-rated movie was sure to take his mind off Sara Jane for a little while.

He dug the tubes out of his underwear drawer and put them back into the TV set. The old set warmed as slowly as ever, gradually filling the den with the sound of Christmas music. He reached out to switch the channel, but before he could do so, the hundred-voiced TV choir sang a line that made his fingers stop in midair.

"See him in a manger laid whom the angels praise above. . . ."

I saw Jesus today. That's what Sara Jane had said that had started this whole mess. What was so wrong, after all, with a lonesome little kid, even a bad—maybe especially a bad—little lonesome kid wanting some proof that God cared about her? It was not as if she were eleven and needed to face the facts. Maybe Ralph had an idea, after all. Maybe Woodrow could work a little miracle.

He took the hedge clipper out to the backyard and cut so much dried grass and weeds that it took him four or five trips to carry it all in. He dumped his underwear on the bed, put his pillow into the drawer, and covered it with grass. The rest of the grass and weeds he scattered across the living-room floor. He put the drawer on a footstool in front of the Christmas tree. The knobs were showing, so he turned it around. He turned off the blinking lights. The lighting had to be just so, or it wouldn't work. He tried a single candle on the end table. Better. He experimented with the music from the TV in the den until he got it just loud enough to sound sort of mysterious. Then, very carefully, his heart thumping madly against his chest, he lifted the still-sleeping Daniel from his bed, wrapped him in a crib sheet, and laid him in the drawer. When he was satisfied that everything was perfect, he wrapped his own top sheet around himself and went to get Sara Jane.

He shook her and then stepped back near the door. "Sara Jane!" He made his voice strong and slightly spooky. "Sara Jane!" She stirred in her sleep. "Sara Jane Kennington!"

Slowly Sara Jane sat up.

"Sara Jane!" She was looking around trying to figure out, perhaps, where the voice was coming from, so he hiked up his sheet and spread his arms out wide. "Arise!" he commanded. "Arise and follow me!"

Now she saw him—at least she turned and looked straight at him—but when she slid out of bed and padded toward the door, it was as though she were sleepwalking. He turned quickly and led her down the hall. Just as they got to the doorway into the living room, he stepped back and gestured for her to go ahead.

She went on for a few steps and then stopped. He watched her back. Her thin little body was shivering under her pajamas. Her head moved back and forth very slowly. She was taking the whole scene in. And it was beautiful. Even when you knew. Like that painting of the shepherds in the dark barn where the only light comes from the manger. The baby had worked his arms and legs loose from the sheet and was waving them in the air. Above the angel music you could hear his happy bubbling noises.

"Ohh." Sara Jane let out such a long sigh that her whole body shuddered. "Ohhh." She dared a tiny step forward. "Hi, Jesus," she said.

There was something so quiet, so pure, about the way she said it that it went straight through to Woodrow's stomach. He found he was shaking all over. Why was he so cold and scared? He had fooled her, hadn't he? He ought to be feeling proud, not sick to his stomach.

Sara Jane took another step toward the baby. Now what was he supposed to do? He hadn't given any thought to what he should do *after* the miracle. Stupid. Stupid. Stupid. He reached out to stop her from going any farther and stumbled over his sheet. "Oh, hell!"

She turned around, half afraid, half puzzled. "Whoodrow?"

"Don't be scared, Sara Jane. It's just me." He disentangled himself from the sheet. "Stoopid old Whoodrow." The choir from the den launched into a series of hallelujahs. "Oh, shut up!"

Sara Jane in the candlelight might have been a little princess waking from an enchanted sleep. Finally, she cocked her head. "Is that the TV?" she asked.

"Yeah." He turned on the 150-watt reading lamp. "I fixed it."

She blinked a moment in the brightness, and then marched over to the fake manger. "That's Daniel in there."

"Yeah." He was beginning to feel hot. "I was trying to fool you." He flopped heavily to the couch. "Sara Jane, for your future information, nobody should go around trying to fake miracles. First, I broke the TV so you wouldn't be religious, and then I fixed all this junk"—he waved his arm around the room—"so you would. Go ahead. Say it. I'm stoopid."

She came over to the couch and ducked her head so she could look up into his face. "This wasn't stoopid," she said. "I liked it."

She must not understand what he was trying to say. He repeated himself. "I was the one that broke the TV set in the first place."

"Huh?"

"I couldn't stand you praying and acting good all the time."

She looked surprised. "I thought you wanted me to be good, Whoodrow. You used to hate me when I was bad."

"I never hated you. Honest."

"Well"—she sighed her old weary sigh—"Mommy and Daddy did. They wouldn't have got a new one if they liked the old one."

His shame began to shift in the direction of the old exasperation. "Sara Jane Kennington, do you think they stopped liking me when you were born? Maybe they loved me even better than before."

"Really?" He thought she was going to smile, but instead her face clouded up. "Well, I know for sure God hates me. I been so bad." Her chin began to quiver. "I know for sure God hates me."

"Sara Jane. God is crazy about you."

First her eyebrow went up; then she giggled. "You're stoopid, Whoodrow."

"Maybe so," he said. "And then again, maybe not."

When he thought about it later, Woodrow wondered if his miracle had been so fake after all. Ralph's definition of a miracle was something that no one in his right mind would believe. And Ralph, for one, could not believe that Woodrow Kennington had spent Christmas Eve raking grass off his living-room floor while listening happily to his sister sing through practically the entire "Hallelujah Chorus" accompanied by a silver-voiced choir of thousands. In fact, now that Sara Jane was back to normal, he had some trouble believing it himself.

Broken Windows

There was something dreadfully wrong with the Sunday sermon, but Philip, for all his thirty-five years in the pulpit ministry and ten years as senior pastor of prestigious First Church, couldn't put his finger on the trouble. He was sure that if he asked his wife, she would say it was the text. Grace was always generous with constructive criticism. "It's a text for Lent," she would say. On the other hand, Mike, his assistant until last month, would have congratulated Philip on the text, while secretly laughing at him for choosing it. Mike was one of those young men determined to out-Christian the Bible. It was always good for a wealthy downtown church to have a social radical like Mike around, but—Philip sighed despite himself—something of a relief when he went on to become someone else's noisy conscience.

The text in question was Psalm 51, verse 17: "The sacrifices of God are a broken spirit; a broken and a contrite heart, O

God, thou wilt not despise." The older members of the congregation did love to hear the King James, but perhaps it would help him now also to read it in the Revised Standard Version. "The sacrifice acceptable to God," read the RSV, "is a broken spirit; a broken and contrite heart, O God, thou wilt not despise."

Grace would say it was a strange choice for the Sunday before Christmas, but he wouldn't tell her ahead of time. It was better that way. The problem, he knew, was not with the text. It exactly fitted the Christmas story: Zacharias and Elizabeth, Joseph and Mary, the humble shepherds, even the kings of the East—broken and contrite spirits offered up to God. So why wasn't it working? Why was the taste of the words like Shredded Wheat without milk?

He got up, the sermon in his hand, and began to pace the study. Perhaps if he read it aloud: "When Zacharias entered the sanctuary that day to offer up the incense—"

Crash! He ducked instinctively, which was a good thing because he could feel the baseball brush his hair as it flew over. It was stopped by the plaque from the Rotary Club commemorating his presidency. Philip paused only long enough to pick up the ball and then raced out the door.

By the time he got around to the patch of lawn, the children were long gone, of course. The damp grass was full of their damaging footprints, and above, the jagged glass of the study window sparkled in the late afternoon sun.

He allowed himself the luxury of a curse. How many times had he chased children off the last square of grass left to the church? And now the window. There was no one he could get to fix it on a Saturday afternoon, and with Christmas so near, there was probably no way of getting it repaired for a week or more. He was about to return to his study when he realized that the little vandals had left something behind. He walked over to investigate.

Philip picked the object up and immediately regretted doing so. The thing was filthy and gave off a distinct odor. One paw was gone and another going, but Philip could tell that at one time it had passed for a bear. When his own children had been young, they had had teddy bears. Becky had slept with one of the silly things for years.

" 'At's my brother's bear," a voice said. Philip looked down into a runny-nosed face. The boy was about nine or ten; although since his own children were grown, he had trouble guessing ages.

" 'At's my brother's bear," the boy said again, sticking out a skinny arm.

"Just a minute," Philip said. "You're the very person I was looking for."

"Me?"

"Yes, you. What about that window, young man?"

"I don't know nothing about no window. I just come to get my brother's bear."

"Which he dropped while you were running away."

The boy's eyes flickered defensively. "I don't know about no window."

"Well, I think I'll just keep the bear and the baseball until you remember."

"What do you want with that stinking bear?"

Philip coughed. He was beginning to feel like a fine actor caught in a bad play. "You children," he said in a voice that a Shakespearean actor would have envied, "you children have repeatedly been asked not to play on the church lawn. You've ruined what little grass there was, and now you've broken a window."

"I don't know nothing—"

"You said that before. But I should like to talk to your parents about who is to pay for this window you know nothing about."

The boy shrugged. "The preacher never said nothing about us playing here."

"Young man, *I* am the preacher."

"The other one."

He must mean Mike. Of course—Mike would have organized Little League on the church's patch of lawn given half a chance. "That preacher is no longer with us."

The boy snuffled, shifting his weight from foot to foot. Out of the side of his eye, Philip could see a small child half hidden behind the corner of the building. The owner of the bear, no doubt.

"If you want the bear," Philip said loudly, "bring your parents to see me in my office. It's the room," he added, lowering his head toward the boy's, "with the broken window." He straightened, turned, and strode inside, telling himself that the whole problem with the world these days was that children were never made to take responsibility for their actions. Later, as he taped a patch of plastic wrap over the hole, he wondered if he had done the right thing. It did seem small, keeping the little boy's toy, but then again. . . .

He had gone back to the sermon, almost forgetting about the window, when the outside bell rang. He got up impatiently. All the church doors remained locked for security, and when there was no secretary here, it was worse than annoying to have to see who was at the door.

A woman was there with the two boys. "Oh," he said. "Come in."

She hesitated. "Bobby says you got Wayne's bear." She sounded angry.

"Let's talk about it in the office, shall we?" He felt the need for time.

The woman sat perched on the edge of the chair he offered. The children stood close to her.

"The problem," Philip began, "is that the church lawn is really not a public park."

"The other reverend never cared," she said.

"Yes. Well, you see, there isn't enough room. And there are the windows. . . ."

"I don't have no money," she said. "My husband been out of work for weeks and now he's gone. I don't know where." She spoke sharply as though her misfortunes were somehow to be blamed on Philip. "The kids ain't going to have no Christmas as it is. They understand that. But they don't understand why Wayne can't have his bear. That's the meanest thing I ever heard of. Wayne's had that bear since before he could walk." She looked Philip up and down. "Here's this five-year-old kid. His daddy's done took off just before Christmas. He ain't gonna have any Santa Claus. And this big preacher steals his teddy bear. I hope to God that makes you happy."

"Mrs.—Mrs.—I don't want his bear, for heaven's sake."

"Where's that other reverend? Lord, when we was in trouble before, he used to help us out, not steal. . . ."

"Mr. Coates has moved to another congregation."

"So? That figures." She stood up so abruptly that she nearly knocked the two boys over. "I guess you might as well say good-bye to your teddy bear, Wayne. I'm sure the reverend got better things to do than talk to us."

"Now look here, Mrs.—Mrs.—"

"You don't care what my name is!"

"If you'd give me a chance, I would. Just sit down, will you?"

Again she nearly knocked her sons over, but she did sit down.

Philip went over to his desk and got the bear. He took it to the smaller child. "I'm sorry I made you unhappy, Wayne. Here's your bear."

The boy looked at Philip as though he suspected some foul trick and then snatched the bear.

Philip sat down. "Now, Mrs.—"

"Slaytor," she said.

"Mrs. Slaytor. I—we—the church would like very much to know how we might help."

By the time they left, he had given Mrs. Slaytor money out of his own pocket to buy groceries, and as soon as they were gone, he called the head of the service committee and asked her about arranging for presents for the Slaytors' Christmas. "Oh," the woman laughed when he told her a rough outline of what had happened, "some of Mike's Miserables, eh?"

"Mike's what?"

"Mike's Miserables. He was always after us to help them. He had this little pep talk about the church caring for those who lived in 'the shadow of her spire.' We called them Mike's Miserables. Not so poetic, but more descriptive. He had quite a little collection of them."

The Sunday before Christmas was always a wonderful day at First Church. Years before, someone had donated an almost life-sized crèche, which was placed in the left alcove of the huge sanctuary. The figures had been carved out of Philippine mahogany, and a church member had worked out a setting that made the Holy Family appear as though outlined within a cave. A light shone up from the manger into the face of the mother. In the right alcove stood a giant Christmas tree shimmering in white and silver. The choir loft was banked with red poinsettias, and the great candelabra were lit.

The Christmas Sunday sermon went well. Perhaps the little episode with the Slaytors had helped him, Philip thought. They had even come to church that morning, the three of them still looking a bit defiant. All in all, it was a wonderful service. He shook every hand that passed him at the back, and then started across the length of the sanctuary toward the robing room. Something about the crèche light caught his attention. Maybe the bulb was weak. He went over to investigate.

He saw at once that there was an object on top of the light. He could hardly believe his eyes. It was his nose that convinced him. Wayne Slaytor's bear was lying in the manger.

Philip didn't know whether to laugh or to cry. Why? Why? He had been glad to help the Slaytors out—the money—the arrangements—but now he had other things he must do. He tried to think of the bear as a little child's thank-you to God. It didn't work. The bear meant something else.

He took Grace home, got a hurried lunch, and drove back downtown. The bear was in a shopping bag, but its aroma filled the car. The green Buick suddenly seemed very long and very new as it pulled up in front of the dirty brick apartment house. He breathed a prayer and went in.

The Slaytors were on the fourth floor. He climbed the stairs slowly. At sixty he thought of himself as still vigorous, but even so four floors were a bit of exercise. The whole building smelled like Wayne's bear.

Mrs. Slaytor answered his knock. "I—uh—seem to have Wayne's bear again," he said, holding out the bag.

"He tole me he left it at church."

"May I come in?"

"I guess." She stepped back. "Boys, turn off the TV. The reverend's here."

They didn't obey, but they both turned to look at him.

"I brought back your bear, Wayne," Philip said, taking it out of the shopping bag and offering it to the child.

Wayne shrank back, shaking his head.

"Thank the reverend, Wayne."

Wayne just shook his head.

"He don't want it, Reverend," his brother said. "He give it to God."

"Lord, Wayne. God don't want that smelly old bear. Now thank the reverend."

Philip went over and knelt down by the boy's stool. "What's the matter, Wayne?"

The child's eyes filled with tears. He squeaked out something totally unintelligible.

Philip turned to Bobby. "What did he say?"

"He said he want his daddy."

"Oh."

"That's how come he give the bear to God. So as God would send back his daddy for Christmas."

"Lord, Wayne. You better leave God alone. He ain't got time for your foolishness. Ain't that right, Reverend?"

"Well . . ."

"See, Wayne? Reverend know all about God, and he knows God don't mess with people like us. Right, Reverend?"

"Well . . ."

"You just make God mad acting like that. See, the reverend knows I'm right. You can't bribe God with no teddy bear. Right, Reverend?"

"Yes, no!" The woman would drive him wild. He knelt as close to the now-weeping child as he could. "Listen, Wayne," he said softly. "God knows you love that bear, and he knows you love your daddy. He's not mad at you."

The boy cried harder. Words were coming through the sobs, but God alone knew what they were.

God and Bobby, that is. "He wants you to find his daddy and bring him home," Bobby said.

"Me?"

"The other preacher used to do that sometimes."

The next morning Philip began calling—the police, the hospital, the Salvation Army shelter. No one knew anything about Richard Slaytor's whereabouts, although the Salvation Army had met up with him before and promised to keep an eye out. Well, it was the best he could do. There was still the Christmas Eve service to prepare for, and Grace needed him to help complete the preparations at home. The children and their families were coming over Christmas afternoon.

He was working frantically and tardily on his sermon for the evening and had given strict orders that he was not to be disturbed when the boys appeared. He never knew how they got past his secretary, but they did. Bobby had Wayne by the hand, and Wayne was dragging the one-armed bear.

"Didn't find him yet, huh, Reverend?"

"No"—Philip cleared his throat—"I called and called. No one has seen him."

Bobby stepped forward. "We figured you need a picture."

"A picture?"

"Yeah. How you going to know it's him if you don't have no picture?" The boy handed him a faded snapshot of a smiling young couple at the beach. "That's him." Bobby pointed to the man in swimming trunks. "The other one's my mother."

"I see."

"I done wrote out all the information on the back." He turned the photo over. In smudged pencil Philip read:

> *Mr. Richard Slaytor*
> *3476 Fifth St. Apt. 4-D*
> *Tel. 465-6879*
> *Eyes blue Hair brown Size tall*

"That's so you can identify him."

"I see."

"Wayne want to know if you need the bear back."

"No, no. That's all right, Wayne. I think I can manage without the bear, thank you."

He must be out of his mind. It was nearly dark. He had a midnight service that he wasn't ready for. His wife was having guests for supper. And here he was, walking the city streets, peering into doorways, showing a faded snapshot to drunks. "Do you know this man? Have you seen him lately?"

As he showed the picture, the stench would assault his nostrils. Several times he thought he would surely be sick and would have to turn hurriedly away. He tried bartenders and passersby, and as the evening wore on and he got more desperate, he approached the streetwalkers. First, they would flash him their sugar-hard smiles and then sneer when he made clear his mission.

It was so cold, his face hurt. He was tired of walking and bending and begging. There was no kindness in the street. The faces he met were as hard and chilled as the concrete beneath his feet. A damp wind snaked up the sleeves of his overcoat and pierced him through.

"Merry Christmas, Pop!"

He had only time to puzzle over the youngster's greeting before the crashing blow hit his head and he crumpled to the pavement.

His first thought as he woke, the room spinning around him, was that he had died. So, this is what death is like, he was saying to himself matter-of-factly, when the pain surged and he had to blink hard against it. He was lying on a hard, very narrow cot. The smell was that of strong disinfectant, and the sight, when the pain allowed him to look at all, was that of bars. Then the pain surged, and he closed his eyes once more. When the pain ebbed slightly, he began to feel something else. He was dead, all right. He was dead and in Hell, but it was all right. Something—someone—some powerful presence was there with him. He was not afraid—not afraid, that is, of death or of Hell—but strangely afraid of the presence. He was both afraid and not afraid. He wanted to call out, "Who are you? What are you doing here?" But he was silent because he both knew and did not know the answer.

Then there was a voice. A perfectly ordinary human voice that said, "Your wife is here to take you home."

Poor Grace! What must she be thinking? He had called her

once to tell her not to wait supper. Someone helped him to his feet, opened the door of the cage, and supported him down a hall lined with cages into a room so bright with light that he could hardly stand it.

He was dimly aware that there was a woman waiting, but he couldn't bear to open his eyes in that bright place.

"That ain't my husband," the woman's voice said. "My Lord! It's the reverend."

Philip sat down. He had to. He was afraid he might start giggling. He was so tired and his head hurt so much that he wasn't sure he could control himself.

She began to swear at the police. "The poor man got mugged. Look at that bump on his head. Lord, don't you guys ever look before you drag somebody to jail?" She bent over him solicitously. "Don't you know better than to wander round after dark in a neighborhood like this? You could get hurt, Reverend."

He was too tired to reply. The police produced the snapshot with the address on the back. "This was all he had on him. I guess they stole everything else."

"Where'd you get this picture?" she asked Philip.

"The boys—"

"Lord. Lord. You was out looking for Slaytor when they got you, right, Reverend? Did you ever hear the like?" she demanded. "Christmas Eve and the preacher is out looking for some no good man 'cause his baby wants him home for Christmas." She shook her head. "If that don't beat all. We better get you to the emergency room and let them look at that bump."

"No," he said. He was feeling a little more in control. "I've got a midnight service. Just call a taxi and get me back to the church. I'll check with a doctor tomorrow."

He was never able to explain about the service. It might have been the injury, which proved to be a mild concussion, but it couldn't have been only that. As he stood up and looked out over his beautiful, warmly dressed congregation, he saw among them a woman and two little boys and a one-armed bear. He had failed them, but there they were. They had understood. Even Wayne was smiling up at him, waiting to hear the Christmas story of God who not only accepts the sacrifice of a broken and contrite heart, but of God who is himself broken.

He descended into Hell. Philip didn't say so aloud, but suddenly he knew what the words meant. Born in a stinking barn, friend of the poor, the prostitute, the thief—broken at last on a cross. He descended into Hell. And just for a while, maybe for just this once in Philip's usually proper and comfortable life, God had let him be there, too. I know, Philip wanted to cry to those who sat before him, I know what it is. Right, Lord? Didn't you let me see a glimpse of your glory?

Just then Wayne held up the bear and made it wave its one remaining paw toward the pulpit. It was like a great Amen from a heavenly choir. God had not despised his puny little sacrifice. Philip's heart swelled with a joy that had no words except, "Glory, glory, glory, to God in the highest, and on earth peace, good will toward men."